"As you wish.

"You'll come to Tesoro with me." Gianni stood up, scowling at having all choice snatched from him. He wasn't used to being outmaneuvered, but damned if he hadn't been this time. "We leave in three days."

"Three days?" She chewed at her bottom lip and he knew what she was thinking. How could she keep an eye on him from her hotel—wherever that was?

He'd thought the same and there really was only one solution to this entire situation. "You'll stay here."

"Excuse me?"

"We'll need the three days to practice," he told her.

"To practice what?"

His gaze flashed to hers. Finally, there was doubt in her eyes. "Why, to practice being a couple."

"A couple of *what*?"

Her voice hitched higher and Gianni enjoyed her outrage.

"My family will never accept my bringing a stranger along to my new nephew's christening...." He paused for effect, and watching her reaction was entirely worth it when he added, "So for the next week or so, you're going to be my loving fiancée."

* * *

Dear Reader,

I love writing connected stories. It's always fun for a writer to go back and visit characters long after their story's been told. So I had a very good time writing *The Fiancée Caper.* Not only did I absolutely love Gianni and Marie, the hero and heroine, but I also got to revisit Rico King and his wife, Teresa.

In *The Fiancée Caper,* Gianni Coretti, formerly a master jewel thief, finds a former police officer, Marie O'Hara, snooping through his London flat, searching for evidence against him and his family. It's not long before Gianni and Marie strike a bargain—but neither of them is prepared for what will happen once they start "pretending" to be engaged.

I really hope you love this story as much as I do! Please let me know what you think. Come and see me on Facebook.

Happy reading

Maureen

THE FIANCÉE CAPER

———

MAUREEN CHILD

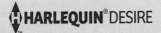

HARLEQUIN®DESIRE

Recycling programs
for this product may
not exist in your area.

ISBN-13: 978-0-373-73330-9

THE FIANCÉE CAPER

Copyright © 2014 by Maureen Child

Printed in U.S.A.

Books by Maureen Child

Harlequin Desire

MAUREEN CHILD

writes for the Harlequin Desire line and can't imagine a better job. Being able to indulge your love for romance, as well as being able to spin stories just the way you want them told is, in a word, perfect.

A seven-time finalist for the prestigious Romance Writers of America RITA® Award, Maureen is the author of more than one hundred romance novels. Her books regularly appear on the bestseller lists and have won several awards, including a Prism, a National Readers' Choice Award, a Colorado Romance Writers Award of Excellence and a Golden Quill.

One of her books, The Soul Collector, was made into a CBS TV movie starring Melissa Gilbert, Bruce Greenwood and Ossie Davis. If you look closely, in the last five minutes of the movie, you'll spot Maureen, who was an extra in the last scene.

Maureen believes that laughter goes hand in hand with love, so her stories are always filled with humor. The many letters she receives assure her that her readers love to laugh as much as she does.

Maureen Child is a native Californian, but has recently moved to the mountains of Utah. She loves a new adventure, though the thought of having to deal with snow for the first time is a little intimidating.

To my son, Jason...who would make a fabulous romance hero!

I love you.

One

"Papa was behind the Van Court emerald theft last week, wasn't he?" Gianni Coretti kept his voice low as he looked across the table at his brother, Paulo.

The other man shrugged, took a sip of his scotch and smiled faintly. "You know Papa."

Gianni scowled and shoved one hand through his hair. That answer was deliberately vague, he told himself. Yet he hadn't really expected anything different. Of course Paulo would side with their father.

Letting his gaze slide from his brother's, Gianni looked out at the well-lit, exquisitely tended lawns of Vinley Hall. Crouched in the heart of Hampshire, on the southern coast of England, the luxury hotel was always the Coretti family's inn of choice—not only for its innate elegance, but also for its convenience to Blackthorn private airfield.

The Corettis never flew commercial.

Today, Gianni was taking his brother to Blackthorn for a short flight to his home in Paris. On the way, of course, they had stopped for a drink. Paulo had been in London visiting for three days and frankly, to Gianni, it had felt like three years. He didn't care for visitors, not even family. And Paulo in particular could push Gianni to the ends of his patience faster than anyone else he knew.

A waitress in a black skirt and smart white shirt made her way across what was once Vinley Hall's library and now served as an elegant bar. In response to her presence, Gianni switched from English to Italian as he reminded his brother, "You and Papa do remember that just a year ago I bargained with Interpol to get us all immunity for past thefts?"

Paulo shuddered visibly and took another sip of scotch before replying in Italian. "Being that close to that many police? Don't know how you managed—or for that matter why you bothered." He set the heavy crystal tumbler down onto the polished oak table and ran his fingertips around the rim. His gaze locked on his brother's. "We didn't ask for immunity."

True. They hadn't asked. But Gianni had secured that promise of safety for them anyway. Unfortunately, his family not only didn't appreciate it, but they were also appalled at the thought of giving up the "family business."

The Corettis had been jewel thieves for centuries. Skills were handed down from one generation to the next. Secrets and tricks of the trade were taught to children who grew into adults with quick hands, quicker minds and the ability to slip in and out of locked doors without leaving a trace of their presence.

There were police on every continent of the globe who would give anything for one iota of evidence against the Corettis. But so far, the family hadn't just been good, they'd been *lucky.* And Gianni was convinced their luck, eventually, would run out.

Try to tell that to a Coretti, though.

"You're serious about this, aren't you?" Paulo asked.

"About what?" Irritation colored Gianni's tone.

Paulo snorted. "This new life of honesty and goodness, of course."

That irritation inside him flared brighter. "You make it sound as if I'm becoming a—" he paused to think of the best way to put it "—Boy Scout."

Laughing, Paulo asked, "Aren't you?"

For a year they had been talking about this and still his brother and father didn't understand Gianni's decision. But then, he told himself, it was hardly surprising. A legacy of thievery didn't usually lend itself to suddenly becoming a law-abiding citizen. But Gianni had had an epiphany of sorts more than a year ago.

His sister, Teresa, thank the gods, understood, because she had chosen years ago to leave behind their family traditions. But Teresa was the only one to understand, because the changes he had made to his life had not only perplexed most of his family, but also, at times, himself.

"You have a *job* now, Gianni." Paulo gave a dramatic shudder again as if the very thought of being employed shook him to his soul. "Corettis do not *have* jobs. We *go* on jobs. There is a difference."

Across the room, a fire burned in a stone hearth, casting flickering shadows on the oak-paneled walls. Outside the casement windows, stately trees rattled their leaves in the near constant English wind. It was a perfectly pleasant room that normally he would have enjoyed. If he weren't faced with talking to his hardheaded brother.

"And that difference could send my family to prison."

"It hasn't yet," Paulo reminded him with a smug smile.

No, it hadn't. But Dominick Coretti—Gianni's father—was getting older. And even the best of men lost some of their skills with age. Not that Nick would ever admit to such a thing. So Gianni had arranged for his father's safety because there was simply no chance his papa would survive a prison sentence.

Of course, that hadn't been the only reason Gianni had, as his father continued to phrase it, "betrayed his very heritage." While being a world-renowned thief had its perks, it also wasn't without its downsides. For example, having to look over your shoulder your entire life.

Gianni wanted something else.

And if his father and brother kept screwing up, Gianni's future was in jeopardy, too. In spite of the deal he'd made with certain agents of Interpol, if it was proven that the Coretti family was still making off with the jewels of Europe, he had no doubt that his deal would be broken and that his new "friends" would find a way to lump him in with his family.

"You worry too much, Gianni," Paulo offered. "We are Corettis."

"I know who we are, Paulo."

"Do you?" Tipping his head to one side, the other man studied Gianni for a long moment before saying, "I think you've forgotten. And when you finally remember, you will leave this new life of yours behind—eagerly."

Gianni finished his own drink, then stared at his brother. "I know exactly who I am. Who we *all* are. I gave my word in exchange for the immunity, Paulo."

He snorted again. "To the police."

As if that didn't matter.

"It's my *word*," Gianni growled. "And the deal I struck with Interpol only includes past crimes. If you or Papa are caught now…"

"Again you worry." Paulo shook his head. "We will not be caught. We are never caught. Besides, you know Papa. He could no more stop stealing than he could stop breathing."

"I know." Gianni wished he could order another scotch. But once Paulo was on the plane to Paris, he himself would be driving back to his home in Mayfair. And he really didn't need a cop pulling him over for weaving along the streets.

His expression must have been easy to read since Paulo laughed again. "Papa is who he is, Gianni. Also, Lady Van Court was practically begging someone to take those stones."

And the ease of the job would have been impossible for his father to resist. With a sigh, he said, "When you see him, tell Papa to lay low for a while at least until the reporters move on from covering the theft. In fact, if you have to, lock him in the closet at your place."

Paulo laughed, finished his scotch and set the glass down again before standing. "I won't even respond to that last idea, as we both know that it would take more than a simple lock to hold our father when he doesn't wish to be held."

"True enough," Gianni mumbled. He stood up and followed his brother out the door and along the gravel drive to Gianni's car. The airport was a short drive from the inn and all too soon, the brothers were standing on the tarmac with an icy British wind buffeting them.

"Watch your back out there in the world of respectability, brother," Paulo said.

"Watch your own," Gianni told him, pulling his brother in for a hard, brief hug. "And Papa's as well."

"Always," Paulo assured him, then picked up his bag, turned and headed for the private jet waiting for him.

Gianni didn't stay to watch the plane take off. Instead, he walked back to his car and drove home to his new life.

"So," Marie O'Hara whispered into the darkened silence, "clearly, crime pays pretty well."

She was in a position to know, since she was, at the moment, sneaking through the private lair of one of the world's most notorious jewel thieves. Her stomach jumped with nerves and breathing wasn't easy. All of her life, she'd followed the rules, obeyed the law, and tonight, she'd thrown all of that away for a chance at justice. Sadly, that thought didn't help the nerves much. But she was here now and she was determined to search the place quickly and thoroughly.

After following Gianni Coretti for weeks, studying his habits, she was fairly sure the man would be gone for hours, but there was no sense in taking chances.

Marie didn't turn on any lights; she didn't want to risk it. Though the chances of neighbors spotting her slinking through his apartment were slim to none. Gianni Coretti's luxury flat was a tenth-floor penthouse with a spectacular view of London. There was a glass wall of windows displaying that view and letting in enough moonlight that lamps weren't really necessary anyway.

"It's pretty but it's more like a contemporary museum than a home," Marie murmured as she walked across the gleaming, white marble floor. The whole place was white. It was like walking through a marshmallow, except it had too many sharp angles and harsh lines to be that soft and comfy. Shaking her head, she left the sterile, if beautiful, living room behind and continued on through a long hall. The marble ran throughout the flat and her heels made light, quick taps on its surface. She winced at every tiny sound as if it were a bullhorn announcing her presence.

Her short black skirt, sky-high heels and red silk shirt weren't exactly designed for stealth. But she'd had to get past the security guard/doorman and she'd had to dress the part of one of Coretti's many assignations. That was lowering, but it had gotten her past the thief's first line of defense.

The kitchen was as austere and off-putting as the rest of the place. It looked as though it had never been used—restaurant-grade stove and sub-zero fridge notwithstanding. Just off that kitchen was a dining room with a—*surprise*—glass table, surrounded by six ghost chairs, so that it looked as though there was nothing there even though it took up quite a bit of room.

Shaking her head at the fact that the wrong people had all the money, Marie moved on, headed past two guest rooms and straight for the master bedroom. The closer she got, the faster nerves swam in the pit of her stomach. Marie really didn't have the breaking-and-entering personality at all. Unlike the man who owned this palace of white, glass and chrome.

"Honestly, would it *kill* him to have a little warmth in here?" Her voice seemed to reverberate through the empty flat, making the whole place seem a little creepy.

Shaking her head at her own errant thoughts, she told herself to focus on the reason for this little enterprise. She

was there to find something she could use against Gianni Coretti. *Sure. No problem.* Police around the world
had been trying and failing to get evidence against the
Coretti family for years. Yet, she reminded herself, she
already had one very interesting piece she knew would
get Gianni's attention. It had been luck, pure and simple,
but sometimes luck was enough.

She just wanted a little…*more*. More was better, especially since she was planning something that most people
would consider crazy.

"It's not crazy, though," she assured herself aloud.
Creepy or not, she'd rather have the sound of her own
voice echoing back at her than the strained silence in this
white, ultramodern palace.

The master bedroom also had a wall of glass affording a view of a tenth-floor terrace and the spectacular
sweep of nighttime London. Everything in the room was
white again, of course.

The oversized bed was against one wall, facing a huge
flat-screen TV that hung over a wide fireplace. There
were built-in dressers and a walk-in closet and an attached bath that boasted miles of white tile, a bathtub
that looked like a gigantic white canoe and a waterfall
setup in lieu of a shower.

She might not love all of the white, but Marie could
appreciate the luxury of the place even though the style
was nothing she would have picked. "You're not here to
be a decorator, Marie," she told herself firmly.

Turning to the closet, she looked through everything
quickly, neatly. She didn't want Coretti to know anyone
had been here. She checked pockets of coats, jackets
and slacks. At least the man had taste when it came to
clothes. She rifled through drawers and tried not to no-

tice that the thief in question preferred black silk boxers. *So not the issue.*

When she found nothing, she went down on her knees to look under the bed. Everyone hid things under their beds, didn't they? She spotted a flat, long box and grinned.

"Secrets, Coretti?" she whispered, stretching out on the floor to reach one arm out for it. Her fingernails scraped along the side of the wooden box and she frowned, scooting closer, wedging herself farther under the bed.

Suddenly she went still. *Was that a noise?* Marie held her breath and waited one second. Two. Then she told herself it was just the nerves battering at her mind and heart. Everything was fine. She was alone in this cold palace. And she was just moments away from discovering whatever it was Gianni Coretti thought was worth hiding. *A little farther and...got it!* She drew the box closer and whispered, "So what am I going to find in there?"

"The question is," a deep voice announced from somewhere behind her, "what is it *I've* found?"

Marie only had a second to shriek in surprise before two strong hands grabbed hold of her ankles and yanked her away from the bed.

Gianni had known the moment he entered his flat that he wasn't alone. Call it a sixth sense. Call it an ingrained survival instinct, whichever. He'd *felt* the difference in the place immediately and had slipped effortlessly into the kind of moves he'd left behind him more than a year ago.

Well, *thought* he'd left behind him. Seemed lifelong

skills never really left you. He moved through the apartment without a sound, his body nearly liquid in the way he slipped past furniture and along the walls, blending into shadows. Moonlight slid through the rooms, painting walls and floors in shades of ivory and cream. Gianni listened, tuning his ears to the slightest sound. A whisper of clothing. An unguarded sigh. A scuff of shoes on the floor.

He didn't so much as glance at the wall of windows as he passed, not noticing his own reflection stalking along with him. He moved through familiar rooms and felt that tingle of awareness bubble inside like fine champagne. He focused and followed the instincts clamoring inside him.

The hallway seemed longer than usual, since he was forced to pause and check out the guest rooms and the baths. But he knew even as he made that quick inspection that the intruder wasn't there. He couldn't have explained *how* he knew, but again, he felt it in his bones. Instinct, intuition, whatever it was, pulled at him and he went with it, continuing on down the hall to the master bedroom.

He heard her before he saw her. Talking to herself in hushed whispers. Her voice sounded low, throaty, and had him intrigued before he even saw her. Gianni stopped on the threshold and looked down at the woman lying on his floor, with one arm stretched out under the bed.

Not a cop.

No cop he'd ever known was built like that.

He did a quick, appreciative scan. Red silk blouse tucked into a very short, figure-hugging black skirt, long, shapely legs and on her small feet a pair of black, four-inch heels.

Definitely not a cop.

His body stirred with pure appreciation. He wanted a look at her. Not just to discover who she was, but to see if her face was as good as the rest of her.

He bent down, grabbed her ankles and pulled. Her shriek of surprise sounded like music. Not only had he caught his intruder, but there was also the added benefit of sliding her skirt up even higher on her thighs.

Even as that thought registered, though, she twisted in his grasp, yanked free of his grip, pulled her skirt down with one hand and kicked out at him with one of those lethal heels.

"Hey!" Gianni leaped back in time to avoid being impaled.

She scrambled back from him, green eyes wide, her tumble of short, dark red curls falling across her forehead until she shook them back out of her way. Climbing to her feet she braced herself as if readying for a fight and he almost laughed at the idea.

"I'm not going to fight you," he said, voice tight.

The woman laughed and shook her head. "Your mistake."

She made a quick move, sliding toward him, striking out with one hand. If he'd been less prepared, she might have caught him off guard. As it was, Gianni grabbed her hand, spun her around, then gave her a push that sent her sprawling across his bed.

Before she could even think about moving, Gianni straddled her hips, pinning her to the wide mattress.

"Get off of me!" Her voice was loud and commanding and clearly American.

Her eyes fired green ice at him and maybe that tone of hers would have worked on someone less motivated. But he wasn't giving an inch. Not until he had some answers.

"You're not going anywhere. Not just yet anyway," he told her, dropping his hands onto her shoulders when she started to buck and writhe in an effort to roll him off of her. At the same time, she lifted one knee and slammed it into his back.

"That's enough of that," he ordered.

"Stop me," she challenged, fighting his grip on her shoulders even as she continued to twist beneath him.

"Don't think I will," he said, his voice dropping to a low rumble. "In fact, I'm actually *enjoying* all of the writhing you're doing."

Well, that did it. As if he'd tossed a bucket of ice water on her, she went completely still. And a good job it was, he told himself, since his body was hard and getting harder. It wasn't every day he had a gorgeous stranger beneath him and apparently, his groin was proud to show appreciation for the moment.

Her eyes were still flashing fury. Her breathing was fast and had her high, full breasts rising and falling in a temptation of movement that captured his complete attention. The red silk blouse she wore boasted tiny ivory buttons that were even now slipping free. *Tempting,* he mused, then forced his mind to focus more on the woman—intruder—than the delectable body beneath him.

"Good," he said. "Now that you've calmed down, you can tell me what you're doing in my home."

"Get off of me, then we'll talk," she said through clenched teeth.

Gianni laughed. "Do I actually *look* that stupid?" Shaking his head he asked again, "What are you doing here?"

She huffed out a breath, thought for a moment, then

tried for sultry as she said, "I was waiting for you. I thought we could…party."

Amused and intrigued, Gianni watched her face and could see the calculation in her eyes. "Did you?"

It was a second or two before she grumbled something unintelligible and admitted, "Fine. No, I didn't."

A shame, he thought wryly. Finding a woman under his bed was nearly as tempting as finding one *in* his bed. Especially when she looked like *this* woman. But lust aside, he needed to know how she had gotten into his flat and, more importantly, what the hell she was doing there.

"If you're not here for my company, then why are you here? What is it you're after?"

She didn't speak, merely glared at him, which Gianni told himself, she wouldn't be doing if she knew how that flash of passion in those green eyes of hers was affecting him. It had been some time since merely *looking* at a woman had his blood burning and his groin aching. But this one had something special. Perhaps it was the fierce expression on such a short and curvy body. Or perhaps it was just that he'd been too long without a woman.

"Nothing to say then?" he asked. "Then let me explain for you. The only possible explanation for your presence here tonight is that you're a thief. A lovely one to be sure," he added, gaze sweeping across those full breasts before he continued. "But a thief all the same. If you think you will find me more forgiving than most victims of a break-in, I assure you I won't be."

"I didn't break—"

He cut her off mainly because he sensed she wasn't going to tell him the truth anyway. "I'm curious as to how you got into my flat and what you thought you were going to find. And, believe me when I say I will find these answers before you go anywhere, little thief."

Her mouth dropped open. Shaking her head, she choked out a short laugh and stared up at him in complete wonderment. "*You're* the only thief in this room, Coretti."

"Ah," he said, even more interested now. "You know me. So this is not a random burglary."

"It's not a—"

"You are definitely the most well-dressed burglar I have ever seen," he acknowledged with another slow look over her body.

Gritting her teeth, she said, "I'm not a burglar."

"Then you are a small-time thief come to me for lessons? If you know of me and my family, you should also know that we don't take on apprentices and even if we did, let me assure you this is not the way to earn my admiration." Amusement gone from his voice, he snapped out, "Who are you and why exactly are you here?"

"I'm the woman with enough evidence to see your father sent to prison."

All right, Gianni thought coldly. Now she had his attention.

Two

The amused glint in his dark brown eyes disappeared in a flash. Marie took a breath and tried to get her heartbeat to stop racing. Not an easy thing to do now that her "plan" was shot. She hadn't counted on him coming home early and catching her while she snooped. Hadn't planned on him dragging her out from under his bed, then tossing her onto the mattress and taking a scat across her midsection, either. And, she was forced to admit that having his hard, oh-so muscular body pressing down on top of hers felt much better than it should have.

He was taller than she'd thought he would be and boy he smelled good—a subtle blend of spice and man that made her want to take a long deep breath and hold on to it, just to keep that scent inside her. But she wasn't here to be seduced or to allow her own hormones to take over and fan the fires that were flickering within.

Because, she reminded herself, she'd already made that mistake once. She'd allowed a thief to distract her—and she wouldn't do that again.

Damn it. How had this all gone so wrong?

The plan had been to confront him in her own time, in a place of her choosing so that she had the upper hand. Now, she was pretty much at his mercy. And judging by the hard light in his eyes, mercy was going to be in short supply.

So, Marie did what she always did when she was the underdog. She jumped in and went on the offensive. "Get off of me and we'll talk."

"You start talking and I'll get off of you," he countered.

So much for that attempt. Moonlight poured through the wall of windows and slashed across his hard features like a silvery warning light. What should have been soft and romantic instead looked somehow ominous, throwing his eyes and the grim slash of his mouth into shadow.

Marie took a breath—shallow though it was—and braced herself for the confrontation she'd been working toward for months. All of her careful plans had crumbled underneath her simply because he'd come home early for probably the first time in his entire life. If you thought about it, this was really all *his* fault.

Her attitude slapped back into place at that thought and she shifted beneath him, shooting him an angry glare. "It's hard to breathe with you *sitting* on me."

He didn't budge. "Then you should speak quickly. What evidence do you have against my father?"

Clearly, she'd lost this round.

"A photo."

He snorted. "A photograph? Please, Ms. Whoever-you-are. You'll have to do better than that. Everyone knows photos are too easily digitally retouched these days to mean anything."

"This one hasn't been," she assured him. She hadn't had to retouch anything. "It's a little dark maybe, but you can see your father clearly enough."

She wouldn't have thought it possible, but his features went even colder and more remote than they had been. And if possible, he became even more good-looking. "I'm supposed to take your word for this? I don't even know your name."

"It's Marie. Marie O'Hara."

He eased up on her diaphragm just enough to allow her a deep breath and Marie appreciated it.

"That's a start," he said tightly. "Keep talking. How do you know me? My family?"

"You're not serious, right?" she asked, stunned that he could even ask that question.

The Coretti family had been the focus of speculation for decades. Catching one of them in the act of relieving someone of their jewels was a recurring dream of police officers around the globe. That he could even ask that question was ridiculous.

"You're the Corettis. The most infamous family of jewel thieves in the world."

His jaw flexed as though he were grinding his teeth. Good thing? Bad? Didn't matter.

"Alleged jewel thieves," he corrected, gaze fixed with hers. "We've never been charged with a crime."

"Because there was never any evidence," she said. "Until now."

That muscle in his jaw ticked continuously now. "You're bluffing."

She met his gaze. "I don't bluff."

He studied her for so long, Marie was sure he could have given a pore-by-pore description of her. But finally, he shook his head and asked, "Why should I believe anything a woman I caught breaking and entering has to say?"

"I didn't *break*," she reminded him. "I just entered."

Fascinating really, to watch his eyes narrow until they were slits even as the muscle in his jaw twitched furiously.

His next question addressed the anger obviously churning inside him. "What do you mean you just entered? How did you get in here?"

She snorted at the seriousness of his expression. "Seriously? All it took was a short skirt and very high heels and your doorman practically bowed me into the elevator." Marie remembered the lascivious glint in the man's eyes and she knew that she wasn't the first of Gianni Coretti's women to be given that special treatment. "He didn't even ask for ID. He assured me no key was required to let myself in since he keyed me in to the one elevator that goes only to your penthouse apartment. He wasn't even surprised to find I was there when you weren't home. Apparently there's a constant stream of women running in and out of this apartment."

He frowned a little at that and she had the satisfaction of knowing that she'd scored a point—however small—against him. She needed that. For what she had to do, it was necessary to have Gianni Coretti on board. Marie hated knowing that she required a thief's assistance, but without him, she would never be able to do what she'd come to Europe to do.

"Clearly," he said, "I'm going to have to speak to the doorman."

Seeing the irritation on his face, she smiled. "Oh, I don't know. Seemed to me like you already have him very well trained—escorting your 'companions' to the elevator and allowing them into your apartment—whether you're home or not."

His mouth worked as if he were chewing on words that tasted too bitter to swallow. "Fine. You've made your point. Now explain *why* you're here. I rarely find a guest in my home searching under my bed. So what is it you were looking for?"

"More evidence."

A short, sharp laugh shot from his throat. "*More* evidence?"

She scowled at him. "I have one picture. I wanted more."

His frown deepened. "Why?"

"I need your help."

He laughed.

Still sitting astride her, he threw his head back and roared with laughter. Marie was so stunned, she could only stare up at him and think wildly, *he's even more gorgeous with that wide smile on his face.* She wasn't here to notice the man's obvious attractions, though, so she tried not to notice that his eyes were the rich brown of melted dark chocolate. Or that his mouth was enticing, his jaw was square and freshly shaven. She did *not* want to touch his thick black hair, which was just long enough to curl seductively over his shirt collar.

The heat from his body was sliding down into hers and as he laughed, her body shook in time with his. Her brain fuzzed out a little, but she fought for clarity. No doubt *any* woman would have felt a little…unsteady with Gianni Coretti planted firmly on top of her.

Finally the rolling thunder of his laughter died away and, still shaking his head, he looked down at her. "You need my help. That's brilliant. You invade my home, threaten my family and expect me to *help* you?"

"If you think I'm happy about this, you're wrong," she assured him. Marie hated needing him. But, she told herself, to catch a thief, it was going to *take* a thief.

"And to ensure that I grant you this favor—you, what? Plan a bit of blackmail?"

"You wouldn't have invited me in if I'd simply come to speak to you."

"I don't know," he mused, gaze moving over her face and down to where the tiny buttons on her silk blouse strained against the fabric. "I might have."

She flushed with both irritation and insult. "Despite the way I'm dressed at the moment, I am not one of your bimbos."

One dark eyebrow winged up. "Bimbos?"

"Why so confused?" she asked. "You should know the word since the women you 'date' are walking, sometimes talking—but never at the same time—examples of the word."

His mouth quirked and Marie had another chance to appreciate how a smile affected his features. Really, though, it didn't matter that he was especially gorgeous, or that the heat from his body was absolutely hotter than anything she'd ever felt before. She just had to get past all of that—push it into the darkest corners of her mind, where she would never have to look at it or think about it again.

Because he was a thief.

And she wasn't here to be attracted to the man she needed to help clear her reputation. That would just muddy up a situation that was already plenty murky.

When he started speaking again, she gratefully stopped thinking and concentrated on the moment at hand.

"Fine. You're not a bimbo. You're not a burglar. What exactly are you then?"

She shoved at him again but he was immovable, clearly determined to keep her pinned to his bed like a moth to a corkboard. With his hard body on top of her and the silky cool duvet beneath her, Marie felt both hot and cold—leaning more toward the hot, though, whether she wanted to admit it or not.

"Let's make a deal," she said after a second or two. "I answer one more question then you get off of me."

"You're not really in a position to bargain," he reminded her.

That Italian accent of his flavored every word and when his tone dropped to deep and husky, the accent seemed to get thicker. Which just wasn't fair. His looks? That accent? Heck, maybe he didn't steal jewels. Women probably *tossed* them at him. That irritating thought helped stiffen her spine.

"I have evidence against your father," she reminded him and was instantly sorry she had.

His features went hard and tight and the light in his eyes awakened by laughter died and dissolved into shadows that didn't look particularly friendly.

"So you say." He stopped, thought for a moment and said, "Fine. Tell me who you are and I'll let you up."

"I already did. My name's Marie O'Hara."

"You're American."

She frowned at him. "Yes."

"And? Telling me your name doesn't tell me who you *are*."

Moonlight sifted into the room through the wall of glass on her left and shone in his eyes as he focused on her. "I used to be a cop...."

"Bloody hell." He huffed out a breath, then narrowed his gaze on her. "Used to be?"

"I answered the one question. Let me up and I'll tell you the rest," she said.

"Fine." He shifted off of her and Marie instantly inhaled deeply.

Sitting up, she adjusted the fit of her blouse then tugged the hem of her skirt as far down on her thighs as it could go. Flipping the hair out of her eyes with a toss of her head, she fixed a hard look on him.

"What's a former cop doing in my home?" He pushed off the bed. Shoving both hands into his pockets, he watched her. "Why does she need my help and how did she get evidence against my father?"

Marie scooted off the bed, too. She felt more in control on her own two feet. Of course, that feeling only lasted until she looked into his eyes. No one would take control out of his hands. He practically *oozed* authority. It was, she guessed, an alpha-male quality and he was most definitely alpha.

"Explain to me why I shouldn't be calling the police to report an intruder," he said shortly.

She shook her head. "A world-renowned thief calling the police? Ironic."

His lips quirked as he shrugged. "I don't know what you're talking about. I'm a law-abiding citizen. Matter of fact, I work for Interpol."

Marie had known that, but it didn't change anything. A new job for an international police force didn't mitigate how Gianni Coretti had lived his life. How the rest of his family was still living. But she knew how these things worked, too. No doubt Gianni had made some sort of deal with the international authorities—maybe immunity in exchange for his assistance. It wouldn't be the first time that a thief switched sides to save his own hide.

"Well then, go ahead and call the police," she said. "I'm sure they would be very interested in the photo I have of Dominick Coretti slipping out the window of a palazzo in Italy the day before the Van Court family renting that palazzo reported a burglary."

Damn it. It was only through sheer force of will that Gianni managed to keep his features blank and not allow this woman to see what he was feeling. The Van Court emeralds. If this were a bluff, Gianni told himself, it was a damned good one. He knew the Van Court heist was last week. He knew his father had done it. And if she knew it, too, then she no doubt did have a picture of Nick Coretti—which would be enough to land his father in jail.

Gianni looked into the woman's summer green eyes and wished her anywhere but there. For a solid year he had been working on building a new, walking-the-straight-and-narrow life and this one small, curvy woman was flushing it down the drain. Feeling a sharp stab of desire for her was one thing. Allowing her to screw up his and his family's lives was another.

"Let's see it." He walked to the wall switch, impatiently hitting it. Light spilled into the room, scattering the gathered shadows.

"What?"

In the moonlit darkness, Marie O'Hara had been attractive. With the lights on she was amazing. Her eyes were greener, her auburn hair shone like dark fire and the curves beneath the red silk blouse and black skirt were lush and tempting. Everything in him stirred. Didn't seem to matter to his body that this woman was threatening everything he knew. A flash of heat shot through him and settled in his groin.

Ex-cop, he reminded himself and the thought was as good as a dose of ice water. Ex or not, in his experience, once a cop always a cop.

"The picture you claim to have of my father," he said shortly. "I want to see it. Now."

"It's in my purse."

His gaze slid over her quickly. "Which is where?"

"On your couch in the front room."

His eyebrows lifted. Gianni hadn't noticed a woman's purse on the couch. But then the moment he'd stepped into his flat, he'd sensed another's presence and had been focused on discovering the intruder. "Made yourself at home, did you?"

"I was going to pick it up on my way out." She gave him a hard look. "You were supposed to be gone for hours yet."

"Are you expecting an apology for interrupting you?"

She inhaled sharply. "Do you want to see the photo or not?"

Oh, he really didn't. Once he saw the photo, he would have to deal with her. Find a way to shut her up and protect his father. First things first, though. Did she really hold evidence that could be used against his family?

"Let's go."

Stepping back to allow her to walk in front of him—

where he could keep an eye on her—he also took advantage of the view. Cop or no cop, she had a great butt, and thief or no thief, he was still a guy.

He followed her through his house, her high heels clicking against the marble floor like a too-fast heartbeat. Gianni flipped light switches as they went and the house lit up, displaying the clear, cold white walls and furnishings.

"Would it *kill* you to have some color in here?" she muttered.

Frowning, he glanced around. He'd paid a hell of a lot of money for the designer who had put his place together. It might be stark, but— Scowling now, he snapped, "Would-be thief *and* an interior decorator? Is that what's known as multitasking?"

She didn't answer but then he hadn't expected her to.

In the living room, she walked to the sleek, low-slung white sofa and snatched up a tiny black shoulder bag. No wonder he hadn't noticed it. Just big enough to carry an ID and a phone, it had slipped between the cushions with only a narrow piece of the strap showing.

She flipped it open, pulled out her phone and turned it on. A couple of quick button pushes later, she turned the screen toward him and said, "I told you I had it."

Gianni snatched the phone from her, studied the man in the photo and felt everything inside him tighten into knots. It was his father. There was no mistaking Nick Coretti. The only good thing was, the photo was dark and so others might have a harder time identifying the man caught slipping out of a casement window.

"Scroll the screen to the next shot," she said.

Grimly, he did just that. In the second photo he saw Nick easing over the edge of the roof to climb down.

His features weren't as clear in this shot, but he was still identifiable. At least to his son.

"This could be anyone," he said tightly, pulling up the menu and hitting Delete on both photos.

"But it's not and we both know it," she countered. "And you needn't have bothered to delete the pictures. I have more copies."

He tossed the phone back to her. "Of course you do. It's as if you think you're in one of those spy movies. All cloak and dagger. Are you enjoying yourself?"

"This is more like *To Catch a Thief,* really," she said and for the first time since he'd pulled her out from under his bed, her mouth curved into a half smile.

He knew which old movie she was talking about and, as it happened, it was one of his favorites. Cary Grant, starring as a jewel thief who ends up not only outwitting the police, but also getting the beautiful girl in the form of Grace Kelly.

"What is it you're up to, Ms. O'Hara?"

"Well, Mr. Coretti," she said, tucking her phone back into her bag, "much like in the movies…I need a thief to catch a thief."

Three

"Explain."

Marie's gaze swept over him in a wink of time. He stood there in his elegantly cut, obviously expensive gray suit, white shirt and fire-engine-red tie and looked like an investment banker. Until you looked into his eyes. That's where the similarities ended. His eyes flashed with cunning, intelligence and a hint of danger that probably had women flocking to him in droves. Even Marie felt that flicker of awareness, of attraction. And she definitely knew better.

"Can I sit down?" she asked.

"Can I stop you?"

"Not really," Marie murmured as she dropped onto the just-as-uncomfortable-as-it-looked sofa. "My feet hurt," she admitted a moment later as she slipped out of her heels and reached down to rub the soles of her feet.

"Well by all means then," he said tightly. "Do be comfortable."

"Not really possible on this couch," she said, running one hand across the fabric. "It has all the give of white steel."

"Shall I fetch you a pillow?"

Marie stopped, looked directly at him and huffed out a breath. "Sorry. Okay, explanation."

"I would appreciate that."

He was being awfully civilized all of a sudden, but Marie wasn't fooled. The truth of what he was feeling was in his eyes. That rich, dark chocolate seemed to be stirring with every emotion possible, all tightly controlled.

Not surprising, she told herself. She'd researched the Coretti family thoroughly over the last several months and everything she'd found on Gianni had led her to believe that he was the one most in control. The one who would go to any lengths to protect his family. The one Coretti most likely to help her. Even if he really didn't want to.

"Okay, I told you that I used to be a cop."

"You did."

Did he just shudder?

"I come from a long line of cops," she said. "My father, uncles, cousins, they all wore the uniform at one time or another."

"Fascinating," he said dryly, that Italian accent of his flavoring the sarcasm. "And how does this affect me and my family?"

"I'm getting to it."

But she was really thirsty. Maybe it was nerves. Maybe she just needed to move around. Maybe it was sitting on the sofa with him perched on the stupid glass coffee table, so close his knees were practically brushing against hers. There was a near electric buzz of heat bouncing between the two of them and it was distracting enough that Marie felt her insides bubble in anticipation.

Irritated at the thought, she jumped to her feet suddenly, jolting a flash of surprise onto Gianni's features. Well, good. She'd hate to think that he was all rigid control when she herself was starting to babble. She only babbled when she was nervous and tonight her nerves were jangling wildly.

"I could use a cup of tea. Do you have tea?"

"I do beg your pardon for being a thoughtless host," he murmured and stood up as well. "And of course I have tea. We're in London."

"Good. Good," she said and started for the kitchen, clutching her phone and tiny bag as if they were lifelines. The awful white marble felt cold against her feet, but at least she was out of the heels that had made her toes ache. He was right behind her. And she couldn't just hear him—she *felt* him.

"Sit down and talk," Gianni said as they walked into the kitchen.

Marie took a seat in one of the ghost chairs, frowning at the clear Plexiglass as she did. "These are really hideous chairs, you know."

"I'll make a note of it," he assured her and filled an electric teakettle—white, of course—at the sink before setting it on the counter and plugging it in to heat. "You're not talking about what I want to hear."

"Right." She took a breath and idly watched him move around the room, getting down mugs and a small *white* teapot. He scooped loose tea into the pot and then leaned both hands onto the white granite countertop and fixed his gaze on her. Waiting.

"I was offered a job as head of security at the Wainwright Hotel in New York several years ago," she said, starting at the beginning in the hopes of keeping everything straight. "I left the force and took the job."

"Kudos," he muttered.

"Yeah. Anyway, everything was fine until a few months ago. That's when Abigail Wainwright was robbed."

"Wainwright." Gianni repeated the name and his brow furrowed as he flipped through what had to be a huge catalogue of information in his brain. At last though, he said, "The Contessa necklace."

"Exactly." Nodding, Marie scooted in the chair, trying to get comfortable, then gave it up and folded her arms on the glass tabletop. It felt cold on her skin, like everything else in this mausoleum, she thought, but it didn't matter. He knew what she was talking about just as she'd known he would.

"Abigail's in her eighties and she's lived in the penthouse of the hotel for the last thirty years." A pang of misery swiped at Marie as she thought of the elegant, sweet older woman. She hadn't deserved to be robbed in her own home, of a necklace that had been in her family for generations. The fact that it had happened on Marie's watch made a bad situation even worse.

That it had happened because Marie had let her guard down made it untenable.

"I didn't steal the necklace, nor did my family," Gianni pointed out and unplugged the teakettle when it began to shriek.

"I didn't say you did," she countered stiffly. "I know who the thief was anyway."

"Is that right?" He poured the boiling water into the teapot, then replaced the lid and set the kettle back onto the counter. "Who?"

"Jean Luc Baptiste."

Marie was watching him carefully so she didn't miss his reaction. Distaste twisted his lips briefly before anger flashed in his eyes. Tugging the knot of his tie loose, he tossed the tie onto the counter, where it landed like a splash of blood against the white granite. Then he unbuttoned his collar and shrugged out of his suit jacket. "I know of him."

Wow. Out of that jacket, his chest looked broad and muscular and way too good. It was easier to ignore the attraction she felt for him when he was all buttoned up and stiff in that beautiful suit. But as she watched him roll up the sleeves of his shirt, baring tanned forearms dusted with dark hair, she had to swallow hard past the knot in her throat.

"Jean Luc," he said, "is sloppy, arrogant and usually finds a woman to dupe into helping him."

At that, Marie had to clench her own jaw and she knew that Gianni enjoyed seeing her irritation.

"Anyway…" Marie said, shoving her unsettling thoughts to the back of her mind. "Jean Luc stayed at the Wainwright Hotel for a couple of weeks and he was… charming."

And oh, how it humiliated her to admit that she had swallowed that charm hook, line and sinker. But was it so surprising? He had been handsome and smooth and so…*French*. He had romanced Marie, sweeping her off her feet, dancing attendance on her, and she had stu-

pidly bought all of it. At least, she reminded herself, she
hadn't been idiot enough to *sleep* with the man. Though
if he'd been there another week or two, she might have.

Gianni snorted. He carried the mugs to the table,
reached back for the teapot and set it down as well before going to a cupboard and grabbing out a package of
cookies. He didn't speak until he was seated at a chair
opposite her. "Jean Luc wouldn't know real charm if it
hit him over the head. And yet, he conned you."

Marie flushed and hated that she could feel that stain
of red heat sweeping over her face. If she felt it then he
could *see* it. Even worse, she hated admitting that Gianni
was right. Marie's entire life had been spent around cops.
Her own father had raised her to have a healthy cynicism
and a low, as he called it, "B.S. meter." That meter usually clanged and gonged whenever someone was trying
to pull one over on her. But Jean Luc had slid beneath
her radar and left her feeling as foolish as any other vic-
tim of a con man. "He did."

"And is he as good a lover as he would have everyone believe?"

Her eyes went wide. "I wouldn't know. That's one
mistake I didn't make."

Chuckling, Gianni mused, "Jean Luc must be losing
his touch. And so," he added before she could say anything to that, "he used you to gain information on your
hotel and security measures. Then he helped himself to
the Contessa and disappeared."

She sighed. "Pretty much."

Shaking his head, Gianni poured them each tea and
asked, "Milk? Sugar?"

"No thanks." She picked up her cup, took a grateful sip
and asked, "Why are you being so nice? Tea? Cookies?"

"No reason we can't be civilized, is there?"

"Oh, no," she agreed wryly. "The cop and the thief sitting at the same table sharing cookies. It's practically a fairy tale."

"They're good cookies," Gianni said, taking one before pushing the package toward her.

After a bite, she had to agree. This was so strange. Not at all as she'd imagined her first meeting with Gianni Coretti going. "Anyway, back to the story."

"Yes, I can't wait to see how it ends."

She frowned at him. In the bright overhead light, his dark brown eyes shone with what might have been humor, but she couldn't be sure. "Abigail didn't blame me for the theft," she said, remembering the older woman's kindness. "But the board of directors did. I was fired."

"Not surprising. You let down your guard to a thief." Gianni leaned back in the chair, then frowned and shifted uncomfortably. "And not, I should add, a very good thief."

"That makes me feel so much better, thanks." Not only had she been conned, but it had also been done by a thief even other thieves didn't respect.

Marie cupped both hands around her mug and let the heat seep into her skin. While she stared across the table at Gianni, she forced herself to admit, "I made a mistake and Abigail paid for it. That's unacceptable to me. I want to get her necklace back. No," she amended, "I *need* to get her necklace back for her."

He gave her a brief, slow nod, as if to acknowledge that he understood the sentiment driving her. But then he started speaking and the moment was lost. "I wish you luck with that."

"I need more than luck," she countered. "I need you."

He laughed shortly, shook his head and then took a sip of his tea before plucking another cookie out of the bag. "And why should I care what you need?"

"Because of that photo."

His features swiftly went blank. "Ah, yes. Your blackmail."

"I prefer the word *extortion*."

"Tomato, to*mah*to."

Ignoring that, Marie took a breath. "I've done my research you know. I left New York right after the robbery. I cashed in my savings, bought a plane ticket to France and I've spent the last few months traveling all over Europe. First I looked for Jean Luc in Paris but didn't find him, obviously—"

"He lives in Monaco."

"See!" She poked a finger at him. "That's one reason why I need you. You know things I don't."

"So very many," he agreed, then frowned and shifted on his seat again.

"Anyway, when I couldn't find Jean Luc, the rat, I realized that I was going to need help." She slumped back against her seat, then straightened up again because the darn thing was so uncomfortable. "Europe's a big place and finding one thief just seemed like an impossible task. But every cop in the world knows about the Corettis and none of you make where you live a secret...."

"Why should we?" He shrugged. "We're not wanted for anything."

She skipped right over that. "I wanted the best and the Coretti family is it."

"And we're all so flattered," he drawled.

"I'll bet." She smiled in spite of his sarcasm because she knew she had his attention. Had had it since the moment he'd seen that picture of his father. "I went to Italy, called in some favors with the force back home and got enough information that I was able to find your father's place."

That muscle in his jaw started ticking again and she noticed that his grip on the mug was tight enough to make his knuckles as white as the rest of this awful apartment.

"Then I followed him."

"You followed my father." His jaw clenched even tighter.

She nodded. "For days. I stayed in a local hotel and learned his routines. He's very sweet. He actually bought me a cup of coffee once in his favorite café. He told me I had a charming accent and wished me a happy vacation in Italy."

Gianni sighed and rolled his eyes.

"Your father's very handsome—he reminds me of someone…."

"George Clooney," Gianni suggested with a tight groan. "My sister calls him an older, shorter, more Italian George Clooney."

Marie smiled at the description. "That's it exactly." Then she studied him for a second. "You must take after your mother."

Gianni smirked. "Very humorous. Does this story of yours have an end?"

"Yes." Back to business, she thought, despite the fact that she was actually beginning to enjoy herself. But she wasn't here to be attracted to or even make small talk with Gianni Coretti and it would be best if she could remember that. Of course, to keep her thoughts from drifting, she'd have to avoid looking into those dark chocolate eyes of his.

"The picture I took was mostly luck," she admitted. "I followed Nick to a party at a nearby palazzo and sat there for an hour, watching the rich and famous coming and going. Finally, after an hour, I was so bored I was about to leave. That's when I noticed your dad on the second-story roof, coming out of the window."

Gianni bit into a cookie with enough force to send crumbs shooting across the table.

Marie smiled. She understood that frustration. She herself had uncles who could on occasion make her furious enough to bite through steel.

"He never saw me and he went straight home from the party." Marie took another long drink of her tea. "I made copies of the picture, stashed the copies in different places and then I came looking for you."

"Why me?" he asked. "Why not my father? Or Paulo?"

"Because you have the most to lose," she said, her gaze locked with his. "I've been following you for the last week, and I think the London cops might be very interested to know just how much time you spend browsing high-end jewelry stores in the city."

His brow furrowed, his eyes narrowed. "I didn't steal anything, I was shopping. For a gift."

"Oh, I don't think your bimbos would know the difference between designer and discount. And as I said, I think the London police would be curious about your interest in the shops."

She could actually see him grinding his teeth together.

"I think the cops have better things to do."

"Possibly," she agreed. "But there's Interpol to think about, isn't there? I know about your deal. You've retired from the business, but your family hasn't. If this photograph gets noticed, your father will go to jail and it's even possible that Interpol could tear up your immunity deal."

"What makes you think so?"

She smiled. "This whole law-abiding thing is so shiny and new for you, Gianni, I don't think it would take much to have the local authorities doubting your devotion to honesty."

He scrubbed one hand across the back of his neck and sighed heavily before meeting her gaze again. "Think you've sewn me up nice and tight, don't you? Fine. Tell me exactly what you want. Be specific."

"I want you to help me find Jean Luc and get the Contessa back for Abigail Wainwright. I want to clear my reputation." She folded her hands together on the clear tabletop. "Once I get that, I give you the photo of your father and disappear from your life."

Gianni took a drink of his tea and wished it were scotch. He was trapped and he knew it. An edge of cold fury slid through his veins like ice water.

First, he didn't like intruders. Second, he hated finding out she'd been following him—and hated even more that he hadn't noticed. Third, his brain kept flashing back to her lying beneath him on his bed and the feel of that curvy body pressed up tightly to him. But mostly, he hated that she was right.

She had him exactly where she wanted him. His new law-abiding-citizen role was so new that London police and even Interpol might look at him with doubts if Marie O'Hara contacted them. He *had* spent a lot of time lately in the city's more prestigious jewelry shops. It would look to the cops as if he were casing the buildings, plotting out their security systems, planning a heist. When in reality he had been trying to find a "new mother" present for his sister.

Gianni couldn't see the police believing that story, though. Even as he sat across from her, distracted by the tumble of dark red curls and sharp green eyes, his mind raced to find a way out. Hell, *any* way out. There simply wasn't one. If he didn't go along with this woman, his father could end up in jail. Nick Coretti would never survive a prison sentence. He was a man used to life's comforts, to the company of women, to the freedom to go when and where he chose. Being locked away would kill his soul and damned if Gianni would allow that to happen.

"I'll take care of it," he blurted out, shifting again and wondering just how the Plexiglass chair with rounded edges was managing to dig into his spine. "I'll recover the Contessa and once I have it, I'll contact you."

"I don't think so." She shook her head and her wonderful hair seemed to dance around her face in a tangle of fiery curls. "I'm not letting you out of my sight until I have that necklace in my hands."

"You come to me for help but you don't trust me?" He snorted derisively.

"You expect me to trust you when I had to blackmail you into helping me?" She smiled, and took another sip of her tea as if she had all the time in the world to enjoy herself. "Used to be a cop, remember?"

He wasn't likely to forget, Gianni thought as irritation clawed at the base of his throat.

"Look," he said, trying to be reasonable and failing, "I have to attend a family gathering on Tesoro Island in a few days. I can't go after Jean Luc until *after* that."

Her eyebrows lifted in surprise. "Fine. I'll go with you."

He sucked in a gulp of air and tried to force the bubble of anger rising inside back down into the pit of his stomach. It was one thing for her to extort his cooperation in a ridiculous theft recovery. It was another entirely for her to expect him to introduce her to his family as a lovely blackmailer.

"This is the baptism of my sister's child. I can't bring a stranger along with me."

Not a flicker of emotion crossed her face. "You'll have to find a way."

His gaze shifted from her to the wall of windows at her back and the dark view of the city beyond the glass. In the distance, he saw the lights on the Millennium Wheel—better known as the London Eye. Any other night, he might have been distracted by the sight. Tonight, though, there were too many thoughts. Too many mental images flashing through his brain.

He couldn't avoid going to Tesoro. Not only would his sister, Teresa, never forgive him for missing her infant son's christening, but there was also going to be a big jewelry show on the island that week and Interpol wanted him there. Gianni smirked to himself at the irony of Interpol wanting a thief there to keep an eye out for other thieves—when Marie O'Hara wanted the same thing.

Taking another sip of the tea he no longer wanted, he silently toasted himself. *Suddenly so very popular.*

Accepting the inevitable, which was a trait that had kept him alive and out of jail too many times to count, Gianni looked at her. "As you wish. You'll come to Tesoro with me and when we leave, we'll fly to Monaco to retrieve your bloody necklace."

"Sounds good to me." She stood up, slipped the long, cross-body strap of her purse over her head and settled it into place. "When do we leave?"

Gianni stood up, too, scowling at having all choice snatched from him. He wasn't used to being outmaneuvered, but damned if he hadn't been this time. "We leave in three days."

"Three days?" She chewed at her bottom lip and he knew what she was thinking. How could she keep an eye on him from her hotel, wherever that was, and prevent him from ditching her?

He'd thought the same and there really was only one solution to this entire situation. "You'll stay here."

"Excuse me?"

"We'll need the three days to practice," he told her, stepping away from the table and giving his chair one last frown.

"To practice what?"

His gaze flashed to hers. Finally, there was doubt, questions in her eyes. Somehow, that made him feel a bit better about all of this. "Why, to practice being a couple."

"A couple of *what?*"

Her voice hitched higher and Gianni enjoyed her outrage.

"My family will never accept my bringing a stranger along to my new nephew's christening—" He paused for effect and watching her reaction was entirely worth it when he added, "So for the next week or so, you're going to be my loving fiancée."

Four

"Fiancée?" Marie repeated the word as if somehow hearing it again would make a difference. It didn't. "Are you crazy?"

"Not at all." He stood with the windows at his back and the city of London spread out behind him, aglow with light and color. "If you want to accompany me to the island, then this is how we do it. My family would never accept my bringing a stranger to a christening—"

"Oh," Marie interrupted, astonished at this whole idea, "but they'll accept that you're engaged to someone they've never heard of?"

He shrugged and the play of muscles across his chest at that action was impressive.

"My family knows nothing about my private life. They'll believe me if I tell them you swept me off my feet."

She laughed shortly. This couldn't be happening. Gianni Coretti's fiancée?

"I don't like the idea of lying to my family," he continued, "but I don't see another way for this to work."

"There's honesty," Marie reminded him.

"You call me a thief and then want honesty?"

Well, he had her there. But she really didn't like the idea of this at all. Not that she'd feel badly about lying in the pursuit of justice, but she was going to be feeling awkward and uncomfortable. Pretending an engagement meant they would have to act as though they were in love—and at the moment, she wasn't sure she even *liked* him.

"Second thoughts?" he asked, folding his arms over his chest and rocking back on his heels, clearly enjoying her discomfort. "It's that police-officer background of yours. Lying comes harder to you people."

"Aren't you the understanding one?"

"So I've been told," he said agreeably. "It doesn't have to be this way. If you'd rather just wait and have me do this on my own—"

"No." She had him with the threat to his father and she knew it. But if she gave him half a chance, he might just disappear and find a way to make his father disappear as well. Then picture or no picture, she wouldn't have any leverage at all. Oh, she could take it to the police, but the Corettis had been avoiding the authorities for decades; they wouldn't have trouble hiding so well they might never be found again.

She couldn't risk it. She had to stay close to him until she had what she came for.

She took a breath. "Like I said, I'm not letting you out of my sight until I have the Contessa back."

"Then," he said, waving one arm out to indicate that she should walk ahead of him, "we should go and get your things from your hotel. We'll have to begin practicing to adore each other." His gaze swept her up and down. "This may take some real acting skills."

"Thanks so much."

He smiled and the curve of his lips tugged at something inside her. Oh, this really wasn't a good idea. She was already attracted to the man—who wouldn't be? Spending more time with him wasn't going to make that attraction any easier to ignore. Look what Jean Luc had romanced her into—and Gianni Coretti was way more dangerous.

Gianni was gorgeous, probably very charming when he put some effort into it. In any other circumstance, she might really enjoy the kind of charade he was talking about. Too bad they were on opposite sides of this situation, she told herself with a small twinge of regret.

She started back down the hall to the living room, but stopped when he caught her arm. That buzz of sensation she'd felt before was back and hotter than ever, the moment he touched her. Marie glanced down at his hand and he immediately let go of her.

"Last chance to change your mind," he said, looking down at her. "Once this begins, we see it through. I won't have my family worried that you're about to throw my father into prison."

His eyes were dark and nearly fathomless, she thought idly, unable to look away from that piercing gaze. A quick jolt of guilt shot through her and then dissipated a moment later. She didn't really want to see Nick Coretti go to prison, either. Yes, he was a thief, but he had been nice to her. She actually winced as that thought danced through her mind. No wonder the board of the Wainwright had fired her.

She was sympathetic to an older thief, had allowed a younger one to romance her and now was desperately attracted to still another.

Maybe, she told herself, this is what having a breakdown felt like.

"I'm not backing out," she told him and squared her shoulders. "I'm in this until it's done."

He nodded and one corner of his mouth tipped up. "Then it's a bargain. We are officially in love."

Marie's stomach took a nosedive as he bent his head toward hers.

"Shall we seal the deal with a kiss?"

"Yeah," she murmured, gaze locked on his lips as they came closer, closer... Quickly, she took a step back and said, "So not necessary."

He grinned and she could have kicked herself. She should have called his bluff and kissed him. Maybe that would have weakened the electricity humming between them. What if it hadn't, though? What if that hum had only grown and kicked off a fire she so wasn't interested in? So, she chickened out and with that action let him know that he'd managed to make her nervous. Not a good way to start. If she weren't careful, he would snatch all the power in this situation and she'd be left stumbling along in his wake. Which, obviously, was unacceptable.

"Darling," he said, feigning hurt, "is that any way to treat the man you love?"

Marie choked on a response. "Really?"

He smirked a little, then amusement drained from his eyes. "This is the only way we can do what you want. Get used to it."

"In public, sure," she said with more bravado than she was feeling at the moment.

"And in private. My family will expect to see a woman who is mad about me. How are your acting skills?"

Sadly, she wouldn't have to act to portray a woman who was deeply in lust. Love might be a stretch but she would pull it off. "I worked undercover as a cop. I can handle it."

"We'll see, won't we?" He took her hand in his and dragged her along behind him on his quick march down the hall to the living room. "Let's get you settled into our love nest so we can start practicing our mutual adoration."

Be still my heart.

They left almost immediately, with Gianni driving them both to Marie's two-star hotel. Like his fancy flat in Mayfair, this hotel, too, was in the city of Westminster. But they might as well have been on different planets. He found a parking space directly in front of the building and Marie just shook her head silently in amazement. No one found parking in London. But it seemed the Coretti luck extended beyond avoiding capture by the law into nearly miraculous parking spots.

She glanced out the passenger side window at her hotel. Funny, but when she had first arrived, she'd found the tiny hotel to be old, but charming. But knowing that *he* was looking at it through appalled eyes put the whole place in a different light.

"'The Prince's A ms'? he asked as he parked out front.

"It's 'Arms,'" she corrected, ignoring the sarcasm in his tone. "The *R* is missing, obviously."

"This building seems to be missing quite a few

things," he pointed out as he stepped out of the car, then walked around to open her door. "Size, convenience, beauty of any sort…"

"Says the man who lives in a palatial iceberg," she muttered.

"It's a prestigious address with a magnificent view," he argued.

"And not a single comfy chair in the place."

He frowned and Marie realized suddenly that he did that a lot. Because of her? Or did he go through life scowling at whomever got in his way?

"I was surprised," he mused quietly, "that the ghost chairs were so uncomfortable. It felt as if there were spikes digging into my back."

She stopped on the street to stare at him. "You never even sat in them before you bought them?"

"I didn't choose them. The decorator did."

"Right." Shaking her head, she turned and headed for the front door of the hotel. How were you supposed to deal with a man who was so rich, he just bought things without even trying them out? He went through life doing whatever he wanted and if it didn't work, he simply tried something else. Hate the ghost chairs? Replace them. Tired of being a thief? Make a deal. He wasn't like everyone else in the world. There were no consequences for men like him.

"You have chairs you don't sit on and walls that are absolutely screaming for some color." Shaking her head, she added, "The only great thing about your house is that view."

He frowned. *Again.*

"If you think I worry what my blackmailer thinks of my home, you would be wrong."

Marie shrugged and tried to ignore the tiny stab of guilt. *Blackmailer.* Wasn't that a nice name for a former cop? But what choice did she have? It wasn't as if he would have volunteered to help her out if she'd simply appeared on his doorstep and asked for it. And she *had* to get that necklace back. Not just for Abby, who had been so nice to her, but for Marie herself. Until she'd returned the Contessa to Abigail Wainwright, Marie would be a failure. And worse, a fool for allowing herself to be romanced into lowering her guard. Well, that thought was enough to stiffen her spine and her resolve.

It didn't matter what she had to put up with to accomplish what she had to. She would pretend to be Gianni's fiancée for the sake of this job. She would act and be convincing. She would pretend to be crazy about him and ignore the very real buzz of sensation she experienced every time she got close to him. She would be the very best fake fiancée the world had ever seen.

And once it was done, she'd go back to New York, and reclaim her life. On her own terms.

He was right behind her as she walked into the lobby of the hotel. She wondered what he thought of the small entry of the clean but shabby place. The hotel was in Westminster, close to the Underground and a little noisier than Marie usually liked. But it was cheap and since, unlike *some* people, her funds weren't unlimited, it had seemed perfect. There were three floors and her room was at the top. Unfortunately, the elevator didn't work, so she turned for the staircase only to hear Gianni behind her, muttering darkly in Italian.

"What did you say?"

He sighed and looked up at her as she was several stairs above him. "I said, you are a stubborn woman to take a room where you must climb stairs like a goat going up a mountain."

"Sorry I couldn't afford the Ritz."

"As am I, *cara*," he said with a slow shake of his head.

Suddenly feeling as if she should apologize for her accommodations, Marie bit back the urge and continued up the narrow staircase. Her hand sliding along the banister, she remembered how when she had first checked in to the hotel, she'd allowed herself to fantasize about the people who had trod these same stairs over the years. The building was several hundred years old and the wooden steps had definite grooves in their centers from the thousands of people who had come and gone before her. Knights? She wondered. Serving girls struggling up and down these same stairs carrying buckets of hot water for fussy guests. Robbers and barons and maybe even secret lovers meeting in an out-of-the-way place. And now, she told herself silently, the cop and the thief.

"You are on the top floor, I suppose."

"Yes." She never stopped moving but her imagination settled into a quiet corner of her mind.

"Of course."

"Really, Gianni? You've been working second-story jobs for years and a few flights of stairs bothers you?"

"I'm not admitting to anything, you understand," he said from behind her, "but if what you are saying is true, then the reward for climbing would have been much greater then than it is now."

She glanced back at him just as light from an old bronze wall sconce slanted across his face. It caught him just right, glancing off his eyes, dazzling them with sparks that looked like gold. His mouth was tight, his jaw clenched, and he was still the most incredible-looking man she'd ever seen.

Oh, this was not going to be easy, she thought, determinedly turning back around to continue up the stairs. When they finally reached her floor, Marie dug her key out of her bag and opened the door. Her room was small, just a bed, a small table, an antique wardrobe, a tiny TV and an electric heater that she'd needed even in August.

"I'll be packed in a minute," she said, thinking it probably wouldn't even take her that long. The last couple of months, she'd been living on the move, going from one hotel to the next in her quest to find the Corettis and get enough evidence on any of them to force Gianni's hand.

Now, she pulled her leather duffel from under the bed, unzipped it and began stuffing in jeans, shirts and underwear from the wardrobe shelves. She tucked her favorite pair of sneakers into the bag then and headed to the bathroom to gather up her hair stuff and makeup. Once she had them in the bag as well, she took a last look around the room, and turned to Gianni, who stood at the window, looking down onto the street.

"I'm ready."

He turned to meet her gaze and both dark eyebrows rose. "I'm impressed," he said. "You're the first woman I've ever met who can pack that quickly."

"I've had a lot of practice the last several weeks," she said.

"Ah, yes." He nodded sagely. "On your Coretti hunt."

He walked across the small room, his ridiculously expensive shoes looking completely out of place on the near threadbare rug beneath them. "You're a stubborn, determined woman. I think you're going to make a formidable fiancée."

"Formidable?"

He came closer. So close in fact that she was forced to look up to meet his gaze. So close she could smell his aftershave on every breath. So close that the heat she felt building between them seemed to sizzle temptingly.

"I've learned over the years that a woman with a plan is a dangerous thing."

She didn't feel dangerous. Marie felt…unsteady. Her so-called plan hadn't worked so far and now she was going to be staying at Gianni's house. Pretending to be his fiancée. She would pretty much be allowing him to take control and that didn't make her happy.

"How long have you been doing this?" he asked, dragging her back to the moment at hand.

"Doing what exactly?"

"This." He waved one arm, encompassing the small room. "Traveling across Europe, staying in these places, following my family."

"A couple of months."

One dark eyebrow winged up. "And you can afford all of this…luxury? Security jobs must pay very well in America."

She grabbed the straps of her duffel in one closed fist. "Not as well as stealing, but I do all right."

"Touché." He took the duffel from her and said, "Of course, as my fiancée, the clothing I just watched you packing is unacceptable."

Marie flushed a little. Fine, she didn't have a lot of slinky things with her. In fact, the outfit she was currently wearing was the only real girlie thing she owned at the moment. Traveling nonstop across Europe meant traveling light.

"Too bad, that's all I've got with me."

"Then we will go shopping tomorrow."

"I can't afford your kind of shopping," she said and made a grab for her bag.

"As you're my fiancée, I will be doing the buying."

"I don't think so."

"You will convince no one that we're engaged if you show up on Tesoro wearing faded blue jeans and old sneakers."

Probably true, but she didn't have to like it. "Fine. But when this is done you can keep the clothes."

"Ah, such a generous gesture." He headed for the door. "You will keep them. Give them to the poor if you like, it doesn't matter to me."

She watched him go and waited until she'd counted to ten before following him. This was going to be a real test of both her patience and her self-control.

It seemed to her that the only thing Gianni Coretti *did* care about was his family. Which worked out well for her. So why was she starting to feel that pang of guilt again? They were both only doing what they had to do.

At least they had that much in common.

The following morning over breakfast on the terrace, Gianni said simply, "Tell me about yourself."

She choked on a sip of coffee and when he slapped her on the back, she glared at him. "Thanks so much," she said when she had her breath back.

"No dying until I have the evidence you're holding," he said. Then he picked up his coffee mug and took a long drink. Leaning back in the chair, he smiled to himself. At least this furniture was comfortable. How was it he had never noticed there wasn't an easy spot to sit in his own home?

Possibly because he was so rarely there, he'd yet to try every chair? No matter. When this mess was concluded, he'd be refurnishing the living room and possibly shooting the kitchen chairs.

"What is it you want to know?" Marie was looking at him over the rim of her cup.

"Everything," he said, then added, "Condensed version if you'd be so kind. We must know something of each other before meeting my family."

"This is the 'practice' you were talking about?"

"You can consider it part of that, yes."

"Fine." She set her cup down, but kept her hands curled around the fine china. "I'm the daughter, granddaughter and great-granddaughter of cops."

"My sympathies."

She shot him one irritated glance that amused Gianni no end before she started speaking again. "My mother died when I was four and my father raised me. I had two uncles and three cousins I didn't see much. Mainly it was just my dad and I."

"Was?"

"He died a few years ago," she said, voice dropping to a whisper that unexpectedly shot a frisson of sympathy through Gianni's heart. He didn't want to feel for her. She was here only because she'd forced her way into his and his family's lives. She was threatening everything he loved and yet, seeing that shadow of sorrow in her eyes touched something inside him.

"Anyway," she was saying, taking a deep breath and shedding that cloak of sadness that had dropped over her so suddenly, "after Dad died, my life pretty much became my job and when I lost that…"

"I can understand," he said lightly. "My life revolved around my job for many years and—"

"Your *job?*" she asked. "Really? You considered stealing your *job?*"

"*Stealing* is such a common word," he protested. "As is *job*. I prefer *career* or…*calling.*"

"Oh, that's perfect," she said, shaking her head. "You had a calling to be a master jewel thief."

"Master." He repeated it, then toasted her with his coffee cup. "I do like that word."

"You would."

Chuckling, he drained the last of his coffee and stood up, briefly turning his face skyward to allow the rare English sunlight to caress his skin. When he looked back to her, he smiled because he knew it would annoy her. "Now, if you'll get dressed, we'll go and do that shopping we talked about last night."

"I hate shopping."

"A shame," he said, already heading for the sliding glass door. "I quite enjoy it."

Shopping with Gianni was an eye-opening experience.

People actually *groveled* when he entered a shop. And not just any old shops, either. Only the top designers in the world were good enough for him.

That afternoon, Gianni marched her up and down Bond Street. They hit every single store and left practically swamped with elegant bags topped with tissue, holding clothes that cost enough to buy a small home. Or, they would have been if Gianni hadn't insisted on the shops sending the packages on to his home, thus freeing him up to spend even more money on clothing that Marie couldn't possibly keep.

After the first dozen or so, she stopped looking at prices—not that many of the items were even marked. She assumed that was because in those shops, if you had to ask the price, you couldn't afford it. Gianni had her trying on clothes she normally would never have even looked twice at and every time she did, she was forced to admit the item looked good on her. He had excellent taste and was clearly determined that she look every inch the fiancée of a gazillionaire.

By the time they'd finished buying Ferragamo shoes and matching handbags—he'd insisted on Italian for the leather goods—Marie was ready to drop. She was hungry, her feet hurt and if she had to dress and undress again, she might just remain naked.

"Lunch, darling?" Gianni's voice cut in to her thoughts and she jerked, startled at the sweet, seductiveness in his tone.

For the last couple of hours, Gianni had been "practicing" being her lover. He took every opportunity to hold her hand, stroke her hair or whisper something soft and sexy just loud enough that the people with them could overhear. He'd said that she had to get used to being close to him. To give and receive affection openly. He was Italian, he reminded her, and public displays of such affection came naturally to him and would be expected by his family.

He had her completely on edge. Of course, the fact that she'd hardly slept the night before probably had a lot to do with that. Being in Gianni's guest room was physically a lot more comfortable that her hotel room. But that's where the comfort ended, too. Knowing he was in the next room had tangled her up in knots. Hearing him move around the apartment had only fried every nerve in her body. How was a woman supposed to relax enough to sleep when a man like Gianni was only one wall away?

And how could the absolutely most wrong man she'd ever met be affecting her the way he was? She hadn't been that attracted to a man in…ever. But she couldn't even indulge in a simple little fantasy because it was just crazy. She was blackmailing him for heaven's sake. He was a criminal. The very kind of man she used to arrest and toss into jail without a backward glance.

And yet…

He touched her again, skimming one hand down the length of her arm, and even as Marie jolted in surprise, she felt a wild skitter of heat race through her system in response.

She was trying to get used to him touching her, but frankly this whole day had been overwhelming. Having a man like Gianni focused on her was nerve-wracking. Plus, she'd never liked shopping and the stores they'd been in that day had all made her feel uncomfortable. The woman looking at her now from behind her gilded cash register was only exacerbating that feeling.

Seemingly, like every other salesclerk they'd encountered that day, this one was tall, curvy, with an upswept blond hairdo that made Marie feel completely unkempt. The woman had razor-sharp cheekbones, an innate elegance when she walked and an upper-crust British accent that only heaped more of the barbarian-in-the-city vibes on Marie's head. This was the kind of woman Gianni was probably used to being with. Elegant sophistication bordering on bored. Marie felt more and more like a Cabbage Patch Kid in a cluster of princess dolls. Not to mention that the woman's sharp blue eyes had locked onto Marie's naked ring finger and then delivered silent, but very pithy commentary.

The saleswoman accepted Gianni's black credit card, gave him a simpering smile and shot Marie a glance of pure envy tinged with confusion, as if she were trying to figure out how Marie had landed a guy like Gianni. If the woman knew the real reason she and Gianni were together today, things might have been different. But then that was the point, wasn't it? They were supposed to be acting out their roles. Convincing people, family and strangers alike, that they were a couple wildly in love.

Well, Marie thought, she'd start here. Jump into the role she'd agreed to and surprise Gianni with just how good an actor she really was. She threaded her arm through Gianni's, leaned into him and tipped her head back as if expecting a kiss. He thought she couldn't act? She'd show him. And at the same time, give the saleswoman a bit of a lesson, too.

"I'd love lunch, sweetie. Where shall we go today? Somewhere…private?" Her voice was breathy and her eyes locked on his, so she noticed the flare of something hot in the depths of his dark brown eyes.

"Very tempting, my darling," he whispered, lifting one hand to stroke down her back and over her behind.

Marie tensed and saw amusement flicker in his eyes. He was getting her back. Damn it.

"First, though, I think we'll do some more shopping."

"Great," Marie whispered, trying to sound excited.

"You're a lucky woman," the saleswoman said on a sigh. "Having a boyfriend who loves buying you nice things?"

"He's not my boyfriend," Marie said tightly, reaching back to move his hand off her butt.

"No, I'm her fiancé," he corrected and didn't seem to notice the woman glance at that naked ring finger again. But he did give Marie's butt a little pinch as if to remind her that they were still acting.

So Marie leaned into him even farther, practically rubbing her breasts against him. She smoothed her hand along his chest in a proprietary manner, then let it slide down. Before she reached belt territory, Gianni caught her hand in his and muttered, "Let's just sign this slip, shall we, and go back home for lunch? I can't wait to have you to myself again, my love." As if to emphasize those words for the saleswoman's benefit, he nibbled gently on Marie's knuckles.

Her breath caught, her stomach lurched and heat set up shop a bit lower down her body. The man had a great mouth. His teeth and tongue darted across her skin in only a second or two, but it was enough to shut down her brain and give him the full points for this little encounter.

She'd tried to show him up and he'd ended the contest by shutting her up completely. Now she had a clerk jealous of her, a fake fiancé angry at her and her own body slowly simmering to a full boil.

Five

"I have something for you," Gianni said, dipping into his suit pocket for the small velvet box he'd stashed there before leaving the flat that morning.

"Oh, God," Marie groaned as she reached for her glass of white wine. "Please, nothing else. I've already got enough clothes for ten women. I don't need more."

He smiled as he watched her gulp twenty-year-old sauvignon blanc as if it were tap water. He'd never met a woman quite like her. Most of the females he encountered were only too happy to go on the kind of spending spree he'd taken her on all day. But she had complained throughout, as if having someone spend money on her were physically painful.

And the more pained she became the more enjoyment he took out of the exercise. He'd dressed her as she should be dressed. In bright colors that made her auburn hair shine like dark fire. In tight skirts, deeply veed shirts and sky-high heels that made her legs look even longer than they already were. Hell, Gianni admitted silently, a couple of times, when she'd stepped out of a dressing room, it had taken every ounce of his self-control not to push her back inside and take her there.

Now, he had her at one of the more exclusive restaurants in London and all he could think about was getting her alone so they could "practice" loving each other. He shook his head and gave up trying to figure out why it was that Marie O'Hara was able to push every button he had. She was dangerous. To his future. To his family's freedom. And yet...

The room was quiet, but for the muted conversations going on around them. Tray ceilings with intricate wood carvings dating to the 1500s were overhead and gleamed in the soft glow of crystal chandeliers. The walls were a honey-colored wood and the floor shone with deep, rich warmth.

She was exhausted and he was completely wired. He felt as full of adrenaline as he used to on the eve of a big job. She was tangling him up in knots and that was something Gianni wasn't used to. Women were interchangeable in his world. A blonde, a redhead, a brunette—it had never mattered to him before meeting this one intriguing woman. Always before, if he wanted a woman, he took her, and then he let her go. He never indulged longer than a night or two because, in his experience, more than that caused a woman to get that isn't-this-cozy look in her eyes.

Not Marie, though.

In her brilliant green eyes, all he read was determination. She was going to get what she needed from him and then she would move on. And it struck him that this was the first time in his life that a woman was the one making the plan to leave.

Why did he find that so…interesting?

"May I take your order or do you need a few more minutes?"

Gianni looked up at the young waiter standing beside their table. "We're ready." He closed his menu and said, "Two orders of roast beef, please."

"Right away." The waiter gathered up both menus and hurried off.

"What if I didn't want roast beef?" Marie glared at him from the bench seat beside him. "What if I felt like chicken? Or fish?"

"Then you'd have been disappointed," he said, taking a sip of his wine.

"Do you always have to take control?"

"Isn't that what you try to do?" he countered and rubbed his thumb over the back of the small jewelry box in his hand.

"I'm not a control freak," she argued. "I simply know the right way to do something."

"Ah, me, too," he said, smiling at her obvious frustration. "Now. As I was saying before, I have something for you."

Her eyes narrowed suspiciously. "What?"

"Ah, so eager for surprises, like a child at Christmas." He felt amusement fill him again. She was wonderfully contrary and damned if he wasn't enjoying that. He was so accustomed to women agreeing with him, smiling at him, that having this particular woman shooting daggers at him was refreshing. Exciting.

"I'm not a child—"

"I've noticed."

Her lips thinned. "It's not Christmas and I've had enough surprises today, thanks."

"Always room for one more." He slid the small jewelry box across the table to her.

She went utterly still. If he hadn't seen the slight rise and fall of her really magnificent chest, he might have thought she'd died of shock. Her gaze dropped to the box and she stared at it as if expecting it to rise up like a cobra and strike. Finally, though, she lifted her gaze to his. "A ring?"

"We are engaged after all," he said with a shrug. "And I noticed that last clerk looking at your ring finger."

"It doesn't matter."

"It does matter. It's an important piece of the whole fabrication we're building. I put the ring in my pocket this morning before we left the flat and simply forgot to give it to you."

She looked at the box again and sighed.

"My family will notice even more than the salesclerk did. They will expect you to be wearing my ring. It's all a part of our act, Marie. The role you agreed to play."

Steeling herself, she picked up the small box, flipped it open and gasped. "I can't wear this. It's practically an ice rink!"

Pride reared up inside him. It was a big diamond. One of the biggest he'd ever stolen. But mostly, that ring was a symbol and he'd kept it for that very reason when he should have fenced it a dozen years ago.

"It's exactly the kind of ring I would buy for my fiancée," he told her, plucking the diamond from its velvet bed.

"You mean showy and over-the-top?"

Once again, she baffled and intrigued him. "You are the first woman I have ever heard say that a diamond is too big. Isn't that in the same category as being too thin or too rich? An impossibility?"

"I'm not like most women," she pointed out, shaking her head as she pushed the box back toward him.

"Yes," he agreed. "I've noticed that, as well."

Her gaze narrowed further. "You say you had it at the flat. When did you buy it? Is there another fiancée somewhere in your closet that I should know about? Won't she be furious that you're giving away the ring you bought for her?"

"Oh, I didn't buy it," he assured her.

Her eyes went wide and he found he enjoyed the shock he saw etch itself into her features. "You mean—"

"Such innocence," he mused with a shake of his head. "Even though you know about me and my family, you can still be shocked."

"You stole it."

"Allegedly," he answered. After all, it wouldn't be prudent to give her more ammunition to use against him. "This ring has sentimental value to me."

"And why's that?"

He studied her thoughtfully for a long moment before speaking quietly, his voice low and deep and meant only for her. "If we are to pretend to be lovers, we must know each other, and so that means sharing pieces of our pasts. Yet," he added, his fingers sliding up and down the stem of his wineglass, "I'm in the position of having to worry if my fiancée will spill whatever I tell her to her cop friends."

She actually appeared to be insulted, if that flash in her eyes was anything to go by. Again, she intrigued him. There was so much more to Marie O'Hara than he'd first assumed. He was beginning to get glimpses of the woman beneath the metaphorical badge she wore. And that woman interested him on several different levels. Not the least of which was the desire that pumped through him at the most unexpected moments—such as now.

"What?" she asked, her voice low and furious. "You think I'm taking notes? That I'm wired?"

"I hadn't considered that," he mused, but he was considering it now. It wouldn't be the first time the law had used a beautiful woman to try to get information from him. Of course, those attempts had failed because they'd been such blatant plants.

As if the authorities believed that all they had to do was drop a gorgeous woman in front of him and he would tell her everything. Really? Was it any wonder none of the Corettis had been caught when attempts to catch them were so clumsy?

But this…he could actually see now that she could be undercover. Coming to him with this ridiculous blackmail scheme would naturally get his attention. Was she supposed to use their enforced closeness to dig for more information against him and his family?

Gianni looked into her eyes and wondered, but even as he did, she was talking again and he listened to not only her words, but also the tone of her voice. Just as he watched her body language. He'd learned as a child how to pick out a liar. And the signs he was getting from Marie weren't that of deception.

"I'm not wearing a wire. You can frisk me later if you want to be sure."

Instantly he thought about that. About stripping her

new, white silk blouse from her shoulders, unhooking the lace of her bra and checking her entire body very thoroughly for any trace of a wire planted by the police. As that thought claimed the front of his brain, his body tightened even further and he was grateful that he was sitting down. Walking at the moment would have been painful.

"Frisking you sounds tempting," he said.

Heat zipped across the surface of her eyes before she was able to hide her reaction. And her response only fed the burn inside him. Damn.

"Leaving your searching me aside," she said, voice tight, "why would I repeat anything you tell me?"

"You could be secretly working with the law and this is all an elaborate setup." He didn't think so, but best to get it all out onto the table.

"No one would make up a scenario like this." Astonished she just looked at him through wide eyes. "But if it helps, I'll say it. I'm not working for anyone. And as for my talking to the police, how could I?" She laughed shortly, a sound with zero humor in it, and lifted both hands in a classic shrug. "Even if I tried, no one would believe me. I wouldn't have evidence to back up whatever I said and you would probably tell them I blackmailed you into helping me, so I wouldn't come off looking very good, would I?"

"An eloquent, if lengthy explanation," he said, nodding. He hadn't really thought she was some undercover spy, but it was good to hear it said out loud. "Still, I would prefer simply to have your word that you won't repeat what you hear from me or my family."

Now he'd had the satisfaction of surprising her.

"You would accept my word on that?"

Gianni smiled to himself. She was a cop to her

bones—whether she held that job at the moment or not. Honesty was ingrained into her very soul—current blackmail attempt notwithstanding. He looked into her eyes and saw what he needed to see before answering, "Yes. I would accept your word on it."

She gave him a small smile that felt like a victory. "Then you have it. Whatever we talk about—here or on the island—won't be repeated."

He inclined his head briefly. "With that understanding…" he said, plucking the ring from its velvet bed to study it. He turned it one way then the other, watching as the diamond caught the overhead lights and shone like a small sun in his hand. "I stole this ring twelve years ago. It was the first big job my brother, Paulo, and I pulled on our own."

She sucked in a breath and held it. Gianni knew her honest little soul was cringing from his tales of life in the criminal lane, but to give her her due, she didn't interrupt him.

"We were in Spain," he said, his memories sliding back over the years to a warm summer night in Barcelona. When he and his brother had formed a plan, laid out the strategies and, in one night, declared their independence from the family and shown that they had earned their way into the Coretti legacy.

Every Coretti was raised to the life. As children they were taught to pick locks, to walk without sound, to cross rooflines as easily as most people walked across their back gardens. They learned how to tell diamonds from paste, how to fit in to any situation and how to slide away from pursuit. For generations, the Coretti family had been thieves. The best of the best, and the family business had only grown over the years.

Gianni's sister, Teresa, had been the only Coretti in generations to not embrace the life. She'd always chosen to walk an honest path. With an actual career. None of the family had understood her desires until a year ago, when Gianni had finally come to understand what his sister had known all along. That stealing wasn't the way to live. That taking things from people meant you were taking pieces of their lives, too.

Strangely enough, it had been stealing an antique dagger from the man who turned out to be Teresa's husband that had jolted Gianni into making some personal changes. It had been an epiphany that had left Gianni shaken and willing to rewrite his lifestyle. But most of his family was still out there, and he couldn't risk their freedoms with his choices.

"The woman who lost this ring was lovely. Paulo was quite taken with her as I recall," he mused, remembering.

"But he stole from her anyway," Marie said.

"Of course," Gianni agreed. "It's what we do. There was a long weekend party at her home in the countryside outside Barcelona. To get the lay of the land, Paulo and I crashed the party, mingled with her guests and then helped ourselves to the jewels she kept tucked in a safe in her bedroom. It went beautifully."

"And they didn't suspect you?"

"Why would they?" He smiled, closing his fist around the ring briefly, feeling the sharp edges dig into his palm. "We were just two of hundreds of guests at the party and we were long gone before the police arrived to investigate."

"I don't know whether to be impressed or appalled."

He chuckled, opened his fist and glanced at the ring

again. "I vote impressed. Appalled seems so close-minded."

The waiter appeared tableside, delivered their dinners, then left again. Once they were alone once more, Marie glanced at her plate and grudgingly admitted, "The roast beef does look good."

"It's their specialty," he said. "I come here quite often when I'm in London."

"But you're not in London often."

It wasn't a question. He shrugged, still holding the ring, and watched as she sliced into her beef and took a bite. "No. I spend a lot of time traveling."

"That much I know," she said.

"And you've turned the conversation away from your engagement ring." He held the diamond toward her, waiting for her to take it from him. When she didn't, he simply took her left hand in his and slid the ring home.

"It's not *my* ring. It belongs to that woman in Barcelona."

"Actually, no, it doesn't. It's been mine for twelve years."

"Having it doesn't mean it's yours."

"To my way of thinking, it does." He picked up his own knife and fork and glared at her when she went to take the ring off. "Leave it on, Marie. It's a part of your costume for the little play we'll be putting on for the next week or so. In fact," he added, "think of the ring as paste. Just part of the make-believe."

"Paste." She looked at the ring that took up the entire first knuckle of her ring finger. "I don't know if that will help."

Shaking his head, Gianni told her, "You'll just have to swallow those honest tendencies of yours for the next while. To play the game you want played, you'll have to see more shades of gray than black and white."

But as he watched her, he saw that her features looked troubled and her eyes were wary. He had the distinct impression that Marie O'Hara was far too honest to be able to pull this off.

Marie wasn't sure she could pull this off.

Living with Gianni was more difficult than she'd imagined it would be. For the last few days, they'd spent hours in each other's company every day. It was only at night, when she retreated to the sterile, cold confines of her guest room in his flat, that she had any peace at all. Any time to think. To wonder how she'd gotten herself into this and how she would survive it.

Gianni was sexy, smooth and very charming. Yes, he was a thief—or a reformed one—but there was a lot more to him than that. He was fun. His sense of humor was wry and often self-deprecating, which she found really attractive. He loved going places, seeing things, and that appealed to her as well. He'd taken her on a tour of London, hitting every tourist spot she'd ever heard of and a few she hadn't. They'd seen the royal jewels, the Tower of London and stood outside Buckingham Palace to watch the changing of the guard.

He'd escorted her through Westminster Abbey, Trafalgar Square and down Carnaby Street. They'd had lunch at pubs, dined out at elegant five-star restaurants for dinner and had gone dancing the night before at a private club.

All in all, he was making himself so charming she was finding him desperately difficult to resist. Especially when she wasn't supposed to be resisting him. He took every opportunity to touch her, to hold her hand, brush her hair back from her face. He hadn't kissed her yet and she didn't know if she was relieved by that or not. She supposed they should practice that as well, but Marie had the feeling Gianni didn't need much practice in that department. And kissing him was only going to make her nights feel longer and the days more confusing.

She looked down at the ring on her finger and sighed again. It was huge. And stolen. And it was beginning to feel way too good on her hand.

What did that say about her, she wondered.

Dancing with Gianni the night before, she'd felt that slow slide of heat moving through her system as he held her close and together they swayed to the sultry music soaring around them. The other dancers had disappeared, until it felt as if only the two of them were there in that room.

His hard body pressed along hers, his right hand sliding up and down her spine, his deep brown eyes locked on hers until all she saw of the world were those depths shining with heat and—

"Here you are." Gianni's voice interrupted her thoughts, thank heaven.

She turned from the stone railing and her view of the Thames to face him as he approached. His dark hair ruffled by the wind, he wore a short-sleeved, black-collared shirt, blue jeans and black boots that made him look both amazingly attractive and dangerous. A heady combination.

He was carrying two large cups and handed one to her. "Latte?"

"Thanks."

"So," he asked, standing alongside her at the railing,

"what were you thinking of just then. You looked absolutely fierce."

"Nothing really," she lied and wondered if she should be worried that lying was beginning to come much easier to her. She looked out over the Thames at the other side of the river to where Big Ben and the British parliament buildings stood as a testament to the ages.

"You're still not very good at lying," he said, a smile taking the sting out of his words.

"Thank you. I was just thinking that I was getting too good at it."

"No. You still have honesty shining from your eyes. Shame, really."

Marie laughed and realized he had meant her to when his own smile grew bigger. "Honesty isn't a disease, you know. It's not contagious."

"You should tell my brother—Paulo—that." He braced his elbows on the stone railing and studied the swift moving river in front of them. "Since I made that deal with Interpol, Paulo has kept his distance, as if afraid he, too, might be bitten by the honesty bug that claimed our sister from birth."

"Your sister, Teresa?" she asked, turning her face into the wind to look at him. "The one who lives on Tesoro?"

"Sì," he said softly and there was a tenderness in his smile now that tugged at Marie's heart. "She is my only sister. And from the time she was a girl, she knew she had no desire to be a thief like the rest of us."

"Wow." Marie knew what it was like growing up into a family legacy. Her own family had been in law enforcement forever. She had no idea what they might have thought had she not chosen the same path. "How did your father take that?"

"At first, he was disappointed I think," Gianni said, considering it. "But all he really wanted was for her to be happy. So though he didn't understand, he supported her dreams."

"He sounds like a good father."

Gianni turned to meet her gaze. "He is. He has always been there for us. Since my mother passed away, he is lonely I think, but he never lets on."

"My dad was great, too," she said wistfully, thinking as she always did, just how much she missed her father. "He was so funny. Always made me laugh. Always there to hug me and tell me everything would be all right. Always...*there*. Until he wasn't."

"How long ago did you lose him?"

"Five years," she said. "A drunk driver plowed into his squad car. He died instantly."

"I'm sorry," Gianni said and reached out to take her hand in his.

The heat from his touch settled into her skin and bones and left her feeling comforted...and more. The *more* was what she was worried about.

Keeping her hand tucked into his, he straightened and started walking.

"Where are we going?"

"To my flat to pack. Tomorrow, we leave for Tesoro," he said, glancing down at her.

"Tomorrow?" She would be meeting his family. Playing the role of tender lover and lying to people she hadn't even met yet. Nerves rattled through her quickly and left her knees shaking.

"*Sì*," he said. "It's time. Interpol expects me to be there before the jewelry designer's show to keep an eye on things. And my sister will want me to have time to admire my new nephew."

"Right." Nodding, she told herself that it was best to go and get it started. They would get through the christening, complete Gianni's job for Interpol, then they could find Jean Luc and reclaim the necklace. And then, she would go home. Back to New York.

Funny. The thought of going home didn't sound quite as appealing as it had a few weeks ago.

Six

She wasn't nervous. Not really. She simply couldn't sleep. Big difference.

Marie wandered quietly through the sterile-looking, white-on-white-on-never-ending-white apartment. She'd been there for days and still hadn't gotten used to it. And now that she knew Gianni a little better she couldn't imagine why he liked it. A person's home was supposed to reflect the owner's personality, wasn't it? If that were true, the decorator must never have met Gianni in person.

He was warm and vibrant and alive and this place was void of everything even remotely like that. The only spot in his flat that she felt comfortable was on the terrace, which was where she was headed at the moment.

Marie didn't want to wake Gianni, so she opened the sliding glass door an inch at a time, wincing with every tiny squeak. Since he lived in a tenth-floor penthouse, the wind was wild and immediately reached for her when she opened the door just wide enough to slip through. She didn't care, though—it felt wonderful, that cool slide of air against her skin, lifting her hair, molding the short sleep shirt she wore to her body.

This high, the sounds of the city below were nothing more than a muted roar. The stars were bright, the moon was half-full, a thought that, she considered, made her an optimist, and in the distance, the London Eye shone like a beacon.

The railing around the terrace had been planted with hedges that were bursting with summer color. Pinks and oranges and yellows nestled amid the dark green that felt somehow celebratory. There was a table and chairs—surprisingly comfortable—and Marie skirted around it to stand at the rail looking down on the city.

So much had happened in just a few days. Gianni Coretti kept surprising her, which left her feeling unsteady, off-balance. She'd expected him to be, well, *bad* somehow. He was a thief, after all. But instead, he was warm and funny and kind, too. Just yesterday he'd taken her to the West End, where they'd wandered through cobblestoned streets, and stopped at a sidewalk café for lunch.

Then, Marie remembered, Gianni had surprised her again.

She'd been looking into the window of a boutique shop, while the crowds milled around her. Everyone was busy, hurrying along the sidewalks. The sun peeked in and out of the clouds and a soft breeze blew a crumpled newspaper across the street. Violin music soared—sad, beautiful, an accompaniment to the summer day that swam in the background. Marie hardly noticed, captivated by the chunky, heeled boots she'd spotted in the window.

But her gaze softened, shifted, until she saw the reflection of the people behind her. And that's when she noticed Gianni. He'd stopped beside an old man sitting in an alleyway, playing his violin with an expression of concentrated love on his features. There was an empty bowl for donations in front of him and no one else in the city even seemed to see the old man, who played his heart out on an instrument that looked as old as the man himself.

But Gianni had noticed. Quietly, he dropped a handful of bank notes into the bowl, then stood a moment as if letting the man know his music was appreciated. Then he moved on, heading for Marie, and she quickly turned to smile brightly at him, pretending she hadn't seen. Hadn't witnessed his unexpected act of kindness and generosity.

Now, she couldn't help asking herself, what was she supposed to think about a man like that? He was a thief. He'd spent years of his life stealing from the rich, and yet he took the time to notice an old man in need and do what he could to help.

It had shaken her, she realized. That glimpse into another side of the man she thought she knew. The man she'd assumed him to be. Her entire life, she'd been raised to believe in good and bad, black and white, legal and illegal. There were no shadows in the O'Hara world. Everything was stark. But now she was seeing those shadows and watching as black and white blended into a gray she wasn't used to dealing with.

And he made her feel things she'd never felt before. Things that she really shouldn't be feeling. The ring on her left hand felt suddenly much heavier than it should.

As if it were tugging not only on her ring finger, but also at her soul. She glanced down at the mammoth diamond and it winked at her in the moonlight. *Stolen,* she reminded herself. From a woman in Barcelona. And then kept as a trophy by the thief who even now was taking up way too many of Marie's thoughts.

"Okay," she said softly, "maybe I am nervous."

"No reason to be."

That deep voice coming from behind her startled Marie enough that she actually jumped, then clutched at the base of her throat as she whirled around to face Gianni. "Trying to get me to fall off the edge of your terrace?"

He leaned one shoulder against the frame of the open sliding glass door. His chest was bare and he wore only a pair of black silk sleep pants that rode low on his narrow hips. In the moonlight, the man's skin glowed like old bronze. Well-defined muscles were etched into his chest and the drawstring of the pants he wore was tied so loosely, it would only take the slightest tug to have those pants drop to the floor.

Marie swallowed hard as a wave of heat accompanied that thought and she really hoped the light was dim enough that he couldn't see what he was doing to her.

"The only way you could fall off this terrace," he said, his Italian-flavored voice rumbling over her, "would be to step over the hedges, climb the rail and jump. You're not that nervous, are you?"

"If you come any closer I might be," she muttered thickly.

Desire pumped hot and rich through her veins and she felt a tingle of anticipation set up shop between her thighs. This was so much harder than she'd thought it would be. This whole pretense of closeness was taking on a reality of its own and with it came other feelings that she simply wasn't prepared to face. Breathing was suddenly a battle and as he pushed away from the door frame and walked lazily toward her, his long legs crossing the terrace in just a few carefully measured steps, she knew it wasn't going to get any easier.

Was he that tall when he was dressed?

She managed a deep breath and held it, hoping it would steady her. Instead, it only made her feel even more light-headed. The whole fiancée thing suddenly felt a lot more real. A lot more immediate. A lot more dangerous.

"Just…keep your distance, Coretti."

"Worried, O'Hara?" he asked, that dark, unbelievable voice wrapping itself around her.

What was it about the man's voice that could turn her insides into a puddle of goo? "No, I'm just cautious."

"I'm not interested in cautious," he said. "I'm much more interested in *why* you're feeling so wary."

"Because this—you. Me. Probably not a good idea." Marie backed up a step or two, but there was nowhere to go, really. The terrace just wasn't that big.

"Seems an excellent idea to me. We're both adults. We both know what we want. So what's making you nervous?" he asked, every step bringing him closer.

"At the moment?" She took a breath. "You."

One corner of his mouth tipped up briefly. The wind tossed his hair across his forehead and in the dim lighting, his dark eyes were filled with shadows.

"I think I enjoy making you nervous," he admitted, skirting the edge of the table, relentlessly moving in on her.

"That's great," Marie told him, looking behind her as if expecting to find some secret passage leading directly from the terrace to the inside of the apartment. No such luck. "Happy you're happy."

"We could *both* be happy."

She whipped her head around to look at him. He was so close now, all she had to do was lift one hand and she could trace her fingertips along the sculpted ridges of his muscled chest. And oh, how her fingertips burned to do just that. So she folded her hands into fists at her sides in an effort to curb her impulses.

"And that means…"

He laughed shortly. "You know what it means."

Oh, she really did. And even if her brain hadn't understood exactly what he was talking about, her body surely did. That slow burn had just *whooshed* into an inferno.

"Yeah, I do." She shook her hair back from her face and forced herself to meet his eyes. Oh, she knew that one night with him would leave her *more* than happy. "But not gonna happen."

He lifted one shoulder in a shrug. "Up to you, of course, but we are 'engaged.'"

How easily he dismissed her. One moment using that oh so delicious voice and the heat in his gaze to seduce her, and the next, shrugging it all away as if he weren't bothered by the heat pulsing between them. She didn't know if she should be impressed or insulted. God, why couldn't she do the same with her own wayward thoughts?

"Why are you even awake?"

"I'm a light sleeper. I heard you open the door and go outside. Thought I'd check on you."

"That was…thoughtful."

"Oh, I'm a very thoughtful guy," he agreed. His gaze swept up and down her favorite sleep shirt and she knew what he was seeing. It was black, with two giraffes, stretching their necks up high beside the caption, It's Been a Lo-oo-ong Night.

His lips twitched. "Perhaps we should have spent more time in the lingerie shop today."

Irritated, she folded her arms over the nightgown her father had given her the year he'd died. She was on the graveyard shift that year at Christmas and he'd thought it was funny. Marie had, too, and now she kept it because it was from her dad.

Besides, she didn't want to think about the lingerie shop. Never before had she had a man with her when she picked out bras and panties. Of course, never before had a *man* picked out more than half of what she bought. That was a little unsettling, knowing that no matter what she wore on this trip, he would be able to imagine exactly what kind of underwear she was wearing beneath it.

"So," he said when she didn't speak for several long minutes. "I heard you say you were nervous."

"You shouldn't eavesdrop."

"You shouldn't talk to yourself, so we should both be ashamed," he said. "But back to your case of nerves."

"I'll be fine."

"Are you sure?" He moved in closer and she half wondered if she could just sink into the side of the building.

"Of course I'm sure. I was a little concerned about pretending for your family. But…" She forced a smile. "How hard can it be?"

"Pretending to be my lover?" He winked. "I promise to be very attentive. To do all I can to help you."

That's what she was afraid of. Over the last few

days, they'd been together nearly nonstop—and all of his "attentiveness" had pushed her to the ragged edge. It shouldn't have been like this. Shouldn't have been so hard to keep her mind on the job and her body from whimpering every time he got too close.

Like now.

The wind sighed past her just then and she realized it was cooler now. The last few days had been oddly warm for summer in England, but it seemed things were about to change. And the sudden shift in temperature was a good excuse to run.

"I'm cold," she said, congratulating herself on the lie, since with Gianni looking at her as he was, cold just wasn't an option.

"Bravo."

"What?"

"The lie," he told her. "Said with a straight face. Almost believable."

"Almost?" She lifted her chin, determined to brave it out.

"You're not shivering," he pointed out, "and the gleam in your eye speaks of heat, not a chill."

"Let it go, Gianni," she whispered and took a step forward, hoping he would move back and out of the way.

He didn't.

Instead, he dropped both hands onto her shoulders and held her in place. She was forced to lift her chin to meet his eyes and so her mouth was only a breath away from his.

"I think we should get something out of the way before we leave tomorrow."

Her mouth was dry, her heart hammering in her chest as she forced herself to ask, "What's that?"

"A kiss," he said. His voice dropped into a rumble that seemed to reach out for her and bounce around her chest like some crazed ping-pong ball.

Oh, boy, she really wanted to. Which meant she probably shouldn't. Her gaze briefly dropped to his mouth and his lips curved slightly as if he knew exactly what she was thinking. Dragging her eyes back up to meet his, Marie said softly, "This wasn't part of our bargain."

"Bargains can be renegotiated," he mused, his gaze moving over her face like a caress.

"Into what?" she asked, shaking her head. "This is temporary and we both know it."

"Doesn't mean we can't enjoy ourselves," he countered. "Live in the moment, Marie. You might like it."

She had never lived in the moment. She was all about plans and strategies and worrying about the future. Even when she was a kid, she'd had goals. Marie had focused on those goals, those plans, to the exclusion of everything else. Dating hadn't really been a big part of her life because frankly, she'd never seen the point. Her world was big and full and busy and trying to shoehorn a man into it didn't seem worth the trouble. Especially since she'd never met a man who had even come close to making her want to throw her plans out the window.

Until now, of course.

Gianni had her thinking things so unlike her she hardly recognized the thoughts flying through her own brain. And wouldn't you just know that the first man who made her body sing would be *exactly* the wrong man?

His thumbs moved over her shoulders, and even through the fabric of her night shirt she felt the heat of his touch. He eased her closer and she instinctively leaned forward. Mistake, she told herself. Big mistake.

"You can't pretend intimacy," he said and his breath drifted across her mouth, tempting her to part her lips. "My family will be with us. They will see if we're uncomfortable with each other. They will wonder and we don't want that, do we?"

"I guess not," she said, because she could see his point. They had to look the part or why bother pretending in the first place?

He slid one hand up from her shoulder to thread his fingers up into her hair, cupping the back of her head in his palm. "We should know the taste of each other, Marie. And now is the time."

She didn't speak. Didn't have to. Probably couldn't have, even if she'd wanted to. Her brain wasn't in charge anymore. Her body had the reins and was running with the power. Marie had always believed that being with the wrong man was worse than being alone. She'd had her hormones, her needs, on lockdown for so long, everything inside her was breaking free at once.

Rationally, she knew that Gianni Coretti was the wrong man. But right now, at this moment, he was the *only* man that mattered. She would probably worry about that thought at some point soon. But not now. Now wasn't the time for thinking. Now was all about the *taste* she wanted so badly.

He bent his head and took her mouth with his, and Marie's breath slid from her lungs on a sigh. That soft exhalation fired something in Gianni, because he dropped his hands to her waist and pulled her in so tightly, there was absolutely no doubt that he wanted her as much as she wanted him.

Need fired need and their tongues tangled in a frenzied dance of sensation. She slid her hands up the length of all that warm, golden skin until she was clutching at his shoulders. Heat seemed to radiate from his body and seep into hers. He tangled one hand in her hair, holding her head still while he plundered her mouth, stealing her breath, her resolve, her will.

The taste he gave her was a promise of more and that enticed her. Splintered images crashed through her mind. The two of them, in that huge white bed of his, twisted up in the sheets, skin to skin, hands exploring, bodies melding. Her brain short-circuited, but then she didn't need to think. She only needed to *feel*. Marie gave herself up to the mesmerizing sensations pouring through her because she'd never known anything like it before. They stood locked together at what felt like the top of the world.

He held her tighter, wrapping his arms around her with the strength of a vise, pressing her closer and closer still until she wouldn't have been able to say where his body ended and hers began. He claimed more and gave more. His kiss deepened further, and he groaned as her tongue met his, stroke for stroke. Their breath mingled, their heartbeats thundered in time to a staggering rhythm.

It could have been minutes, or hours. Marie's mind was fuzzed out and her body was burning. The night surrounded them, wrapping them in a cocoon of stars and moon and the cool touch of the wind. The entire world seemed to shrink around them until all that existed was that terrace and the two people on it. It was a moment out of time, and Marie knew that things between she and Gianni would never be the same.

When her head was spinning and her knees were weak, he finally broke the kiss and left Marie swaying slightly until she fell against his chest breathlessly. Her only comfort being that judging from the racing of his heartbeat he was handling this no better than she was.

"That was," he said finally, "a revelation."

She laughed and shook her head against his chest. "A revelation?"

"Yes." He tipped her chin up so that he could peer into her eyes as if searching for something. Then he quipped, "I've never kissed a cop before. I believe I may have been cheating myself all these years."

"Well," she admitted, going for the same falsely light-hearted tone that he'd adopted, "I've never kissed a thief before, either, and I've got to say, it was pretty good."

"Pretty good?" he repeated, laughter in his eyes. "There's putting me in my place."

Smiling up at him, Marie answered, "Who knows? With practice you might get better."

He smoothed her hair back from her face, then trailed his fingertips down her jaw and cupped her cheek. The smile was still in his dark brown eyes when he assured her, "I'm a devil for practice, *cara*. Why settle for pretty good when, with a little hard work, you can have perfection?"

Oh, boy.

The plane ride to St. Thomas felt like it took days.

Gianni was tangled up in knots and he knew it was Marie's fault. There she sat, in her new, designer clothes, and all he could picture was her in that ridiculous giraffe nightshirt. The one that covered her only to the tops of her thighs. The one he'd held pressed so tightly to him he could feel the pebbled hardness of her nipples against his chest.

Her hair was smooth and tangle-free, her makeup was

perfect and yet, his mind held the image of windblown curls, sleepy eyes and a kiss-swollen mouth. Deliberately then, he wiped that image from his mind. He couldn't allow himself to get caught up in this little theatrical production they had going on.

What he had to remember was that this woman was only here because she had threatened his father's freedom. She was blackmailing him and that was hardly the basis for the kind of relationship he'd like to have with her. Sleeping with a woman who had a separate agenda was a dangerous thing.

So he'd keep his distance. Get through this week with his family, then recover her necklace and get the evidence she held against his father. Then he'd walk away—or she would. That's why he was here, after all. To keep his family safe, he would risk everything. Even a week in the same room as Marie O'Hara.

By the time they arrived on Tesoro a couple hours later, Gianni was back in control. He'd used the familiarity of the flight to St. Thomas, and the private boat launch taking them to the island, to smooth out his thoughts again. The trip had become second nature to him in the year that his sister had been living here. The Corettis were a close family and took every chance they had to get together, plus Gianni enjoyed seeing Teresa happy in her new life.

If there were a small thread of trepidation inside him at the idea of bringing Marie into the heart of his family on the strength of a lie, he ignored it.

"It's beautiful."

Gianni turned to face Marie, who was sitting on the sapphire-blue bench seat opposite him. Sunlight poured down on her and lit the dark fire of her hair. The wind tossed that hair into the wild curls he preferred and there was a shine in her eyes as she stared ahead at the island.

It was just the two of them on the launch and yet they hadn't spoken since leaving St. Thomas. There was tension between them now, humming since the night before. His own damn fault, of course. It had been a whim. More of a game than anything else, he told himself. One kiss. To unsettle her. Keep her off balance. But it had become so much more.

He'd never known a single kiss to be so explosive. With that one taste of her, he'd craved more. Like a man dying of thirst and being offered only a swallow of cool water, he'd wanted to gorge himself. He'd almost let himself forget who she was and why she was there. Almost put aside his natural sense of caution to indulge in something that might have ended up endangering the very family he was trying to protect.

It hadn't been easy to deny what was there between them. Pulling away from her had cost him. He'd spent the next several hours in exquisite pain from the ache of denying himself.

So he had no one to blame but himself for what he was feeling now. And damned if he'd let her know that he was still suffering.

"Tesoro is beautiful," he agreed, watching her features rather than the island. He knew what she was seeing. Miles of white beaches, palm trees staggered along the coastline, interspersed with other trees throwing shade across narrow roads and homes with terra-cotta tile roofs jutting out along the cliff lines. He knew the dock would be busy, crowded with local fishing boats and other tourist launches.

"It's like a rainbow on the ground," she said, lifting

her voice over the roar of the boat engine. She turned a smile on him that lit up her face and shone in her eyes.

A hard woman to ignore, he acknowledged, as a jolt of desire rocked him momentarily. Beautiful, he thought, but more than that, she had a mind and a fierce will that really appealed to him on many levels. Too damn bad, really.

"It's a nice place," he said, forcing himself to keep his thoughts on the conversation and to stop taking off on wild tangents that led absolutely nowhere. "Teresa loves it here."

"And you don't?"

"Clever to pick up on that, aren't you?" He nodded and shifted his gaze to the fast-approaching dock. "As a brief holiday, Tesoro is perfect. Wait until you go into the village," he said. "Flowers everywhere, cobbled street, brightly colored shops crowded together."

"Sounds wonderful."

"Oh, it is. But after a week or so, I become restless." He looked at her. "I need the city I think. The bustle. The noise. The sense of life being pursued relentlessly—while here, most are content to allow life to meander along on its own terms."

She nodded thoughtfully. "I've always loved a big city, too. People say they're impersonal, but they're really not. It's just that life is so busy people are too rushed to get involved in each other's lives." Tipping her face up into the sun and the salt spray on the wind, she closed her eyes and added, "Still, friends can be counted on and when you do get the chance to slow down, there's so much to see and feel and experience in a city."

Damn it. She really was close to perfect. But for the whole blackmail issue. And that had to remain at the top of his consciousness. She had come to him with a threat to imprison his father. Their "relationship" was nothing more than a play.

And Gianni found himself regretting that fact a bit more every day.

Seven

"It looks as though we have a welcoming committee," Gianni said when he turned his head to stare at the dock. "That's my sister and her husband, Rico, waiting for us."

"Darn it," she muttered. "Those nerves are back again."

He knew what she meant. Lying as a thief was one thing. Lying to his family was something else again. But what choice did he have, really? If he were to keep his father out of jail, this was necessary. And once it was all over and Marie had gone home to New York, he would explain it all to the Corettis and they'd understand. He hoped.

"It will be fine."

"Easy for you to say," she told him, her gaze still locked on the dock and the two people waiting for them. "You already know them."

"And you know me," he said.

"Do I?" Her startling green gaze shifted to his.

One eyebrow lifted and a smirk curved his mouth briefly. "Really? Is now the time to get into a deep, existential conversation when we are moments from docking?"

"No," she said shortly, and straightened, squaring her shoulders and lifting her chin as if she were preparing to climb the steps of a gallows.

Damned if she weren't the strangest combination of fierce determination and quiet vulnerability. It was all he could do to keep from scooping her up, wrapping his arms around her and just holding on to her until she lost that guarded look in her eyes. Which officially made him *stolto*—foolish. Or worse.

"Good. Because here we are." The boat eased into the slip at dockside and Teresa was shouting.

"Gianni! I'm so glad to see you!" Her black hair was pulled back into a ponytail that somehow made her seem far too young to be a wife and mother. She wore white linen shorts, a red cotton blouse and sandals on her feet.

He jumped out of the boat, clambering onto the dock just in time to catch his baby sister as she threw herself at him. He caught her up and squeezed her hard before setting her onto her feet again.

"Motherhood looks good on you."

"You always know just the right thing to say."

"It's a gift," he said with a wink.

Rico stepped up then and held out one hand. "Good to have you back," he said. "Teresa has been missing her family."

Gianni noticed that even living on a tropical island hadn't altered Rico's wardrobe. He still wore all black, and here on this tropical island he stood out like a funeral director at a wedding.

"You should come to London and visit me. Leave the island once in a while."

"Leave all this?" Teresa laughed and shook her head. "No thank you."

Gianni turned back to the boat, caught Marie's wary gaze and reached out one hand to help her onto the deck. While he did, he noticed that his sister's voice had died away, leaving behind surprised silence. Now the only sounds he heard were from the seagulls flying and screeching overhead, the slap of water against the hull of the launch boat and, from a nearby fishing boat, the muffled sound of someone's radio.

Marie met his gaze and he willed her to relax. His family would expect a certain degree of nervousness, sure. But too much and they might guess that something was up. As if she had understood his concerns, she nodded, took a breath and forced a smile that was good enough to fool Teresa—but not Gianni. He knew her too well. After only a few days, he had learned her expressions, her moods, and he was fascinated by all of her.

"Gianni?" Teresa's voice brought him back from his thoughts and reminded him of where they were and what they were doing.

He gave Marie's fingers a squeeze, then pulled her in close to his side and dropped one arm around her shoulders as he turned to face his family.

"Teresa," he said, "I want you to meet Marie O'Hara."

His sister's eyes shone with confusion, then lit up with excitement when he added, "My fiancée."

"What? Oh, my goodness! This is wonderful!" Teresa shrieked and charged over to envelop Marie in a hard hug. "I'm so happy to meet you! Oh, wow, this is so great. My big brother getting married!" She let go of Marie long enough to throw her arms around Gianni's neck again.

Guilt pinged around inside him like a steel ball in an old-fashioned pinball machine. The feeling only intensified when Teresa whispered in his ear, "This makes me so happy, Gianni. I want you to love and be loved, as I am. I want that for all of my family."

He gave her an extra hard squeeze to compensate for the fact that he now felt like a complete bastard for lying to his little sister. And knowing that today was just the beginning of the charade only made him feel worse. But he was already in it and there was no way out but through it. With that thought in mind, he said, "I'm glad."

Still grinning, Teresa let go of him, then turned back to Marie and linked arms with her. "This is so wonderful, what a happy surprise!" As she drew Marie away from Gianni and headed down the dock toward the hotel, he heard his sister say, "I know we will be great friends, Marie! And now, I want to hear everything. You must tell me how you met and where and oh, we must talk about wedding plans and…"

Marie threw one frantic glance over her shoulder at Gianni, but there was nothing he could do to save her. Once his sister got a head of steam under her, there was simply no stopping her. It was either go along with her or get run over.

Besides, this was good, he told himself. Marie had been thrown into the deep end and she would find a way to swim. The women were getting farther and farther away when Gianni and Rico finally began to walk, too.

"Your sister worries about you and Paulo and your father," Rico mused, his gaze fixed on his wife in the distance. "She thinks you're all alone too much."

Gianni snorted. "We're only alone when we want to be."

Rico chuckled along with him. "That's how I used to be, too, so I understand. But she doesn't. Teresa believes that alone equates with lonely. She doesn't like to think about her family being lonely."

Lonely. Gianni had never considered himself lonely and he knew Paulo didn't think of himself as lonely, either. They lived their own lives on their own terms. They had women when they wanted them and time to themselves otherwise. Hell, Gianni had always avoided having the same woman around him for more than a couple of days at a stretch. In his experience, that kind of closeness infected a woman's mind with dreamy, hazy thoughts of picket fences and dogs and kids. Nothing he had ever been interested in.

And yet, he was forced to admit, the last few days with Marie hadn't bothered him at all. In fact, he'd enjoyed their time together. He frowned to himself at the realization that he wasn't tired of her yet. Wasn't annoyed by her conversation. And he hadn't even slept with her.

Yet.

"I guarantee you by the time we get back to the hotel," Rico was saying, "Teresa will have learned everything there is to know about you and Marie."

Well, there was a sobering thought. Gianni frowned after the two women. Behind him on the boat, the launch pilot was unloading their luggage and setting it onto the dock for the hotel employees to transport.

"Before we catch up to our women," Rico said, drawing to a stop and waiting for Gianni to do the same, "I wanted to talk to you."

Dappled shade fell around them and the ever-present trade winds blew past, carrying the scent of the flowers and the sea with it. Gianni looked at his brother-in-law and waited.

"The jewelry show," Rico said slowly, his eyes narrowed and his jaw tight. "I want your word that the Corettis won't be...*working* this week."

Gianni laughed shortly. He couldn't blame Rico for being cautious. Years ago, Gianni himself had stolen a gold, antique Aztec dagger from Rico's collection. Strangely enough, it had been that very dagger that had brought about the epiphany that had changed Gianni's life.

It was understandable that Rico still had his doubts when even Gianni wondered from time to time if he'd be able to stay on the straight-and-narrow path he had chosen.

"You have my word, Rico," he said. "And I'm speaking for Papa and Paulo as well. You're family now and the Corettis respect family."

Rico nodded. "Good. I don't want any trouble here this week. The top designers in the world have been planning this gathering for nearly a year and I want it to go off without a hitch."

"I'm with you on that," he said. Then he reminded Rico, "Remember I told you that I'm here to do a job for Interpol. To keep an eye on the crowds and look for anything suspicious."

Rico turned and started walking along the dock, with Gianni falling into step beside him. "My security team is the best in the world."

"They're good," Gianni agreed amiably. "I'm better."

Scowling, Rico admitted, "Probably." He shifted his gaze to his wife and Marie walking far ahead of them. "So, engaged. How did that happen?"

Gianni thought about that for a moment. He could lie as he'd meant to. But as his gaze locked on the auburn-haired woman who was, as always, flitting at the edges of his mind, he told the absolute truth.

"She swept me off my feet."

"It was sort of a whirlwind." Marie took a sip of her coffee and mentally kicked herself for agreeing to this whole thing. She was sitting here lying to a really nice woman and she was feeling worse about it by the moment.

Teresa Coretti King was friendly, welcoming and so excited for her brother's "engagement" it made Marie feel even worse than she had thought she would. But she was in it now and there was no getting out. To tell the truth now would be to admit to lying in the first place. And to tell the truth would be to admit to blackmailing Gianni and threatening their father and she was fairly sure Teresa's warm welcome would go out the window at that point. So she kept quiet. Kept smiling, and kept regretting.

She shifted a look around the owners' penthouse suite at the Tesoro Castle, Rico's luxury hotel. The room was incredibly spacious and unlike Gianni's sterile man-cave, this place was filled with bright, primary colors. Sunshine-yellow couches faced each other across a low-slung glass coffee table. There were sapphire-blue and ruby-red throw pillows on the couches and matching chairs. Bamboo floors shone in the sunlight streaming through the open glass windows and a wind scented by tropical flowers flowed in the French doors.

The view was incredible, trees and sandy beaches and wild shrubbery studded with the flowers that seemed to be a part of this incredible place. And then there was the ocean, a deep, beautiful blue that stretched on for miles, while sailboats skimmed the surface.

They'd been on the island for all of an hour and they'd already had a fantastic lunch in the hotel dining room, then come up here, where presumably Teresa could really get to know Marie. And that worried Marie again. The more she talked to the woman the more lies she had to tell and the more questions Teresa asked—it was just a vicious, ugly circle.

"I'm so happy for you two," Teresa said and Marie turned her gaze back to the woman sitting opposite her on one of the two couches. Teresa shifted her two-month-old son, Matteo, in her arms and added, "It's all very romantic, isn't it, Rico?"

Rico scooped Matteo out of his wife's arms and said wryly, "It's fast anyway."

Marie glanced at Gianni and saw him shift uncomfortably in his chair. Good. She was glad he was having a hard time with this, too.

"I don't remember you taking a lot of time when it came to my sister," Gianni murmured and Rico nodded as if acknowledging the statement.

"True," he said.

"Pay no attention to my husband," Teresa said with a mock scowl for Rico. "He thinks now that he's married me, there's no need for romance."

"I romance your socks off and you know it," Rico said, leaning in to kiss his wife, a wicked smile curving his mouth. "Aren't we living here at the hotel while we completely gut our home so that you can redecorate it the way you want?"

She took a breath, sighed it out and said, "All right yes, you are romantic. And indulgent." As an aside, she looked at Marie and said, "We have this lovely house on a hill just beyond the hotel. But Rico was a bachelor when he had it built and now that we're starting a family..." She paused to look at her son. "I wanted the house to be more child-friendly. Rico's cousin, Sean King, lives on the island, too, with his wife, Melinda, and he's brought contractors in to work with the locals on redoing almost everything. Which is why we're living here at the hotel for now."

"She doesn't care about your remodeling issues," Gianni assured his sister.

"Of course she does," Teresa argued. "All women love to redecorate."

"You should send your team to your brother's house when they're finished here," Marie said. "He could use the help."

"Now you're a decorator as well." Gianni's lips twitched. "A Renaissance woman."

"It doesn't take a decorator to know the only comfortable chairs in your house are on the terrace," she countered.

He scowled at her and Teresa laughed with delight. "This is so much fun, Gianni. Watching a woman get the best of you for a change."

Gianni quirked an eyebrow at her. "My house is perfectly serviceable."

"Ah, yes, what all homes should be," Teresa mused with a smile for Marie.

"Our home was serviceable, too," Rico pointed out.

"Exactly!"

They were perfect together, Marie thought and wondered what that was like. How it must feel to know that there was one person in the world who loved you more than anything. Who looked at you as Rico was looking at Teresa now.

"I know! You must get married here on the island," Teresa declared.

Startled at the abrupt change of subject as much as by the subject itself, Marie looked from Teresa to Gianni and back again as the woman continued in a rush.

"Oh! We could do the wedding this week! Papa and Paulo will be here so it would be perfect." Reaching out, she grabbed up a tablet and pen off the coffee table and started making notes to herself.

Rico shrugged. "Teresa has paper and pen all over the hotel—if a new recipe occurs to her, she wants to be able to write it down instantly."

Confused now, Marie looked at Gianni. "My sister decided that instead of becoming a thief, she would become a chef. Naturally, she is wonderful with food."

Teresa looked at him for a long minute, then shifted her gaze to Marie. "You know about the Coretti family then?"

"Yes," Marie told her and felt good having something honest to say. "I know about the master jewel thieves."

Teresa winced, but Gianni chuckled. "Did you think I wouldn't tell her?"

"Of course not," Teresa said, "But I'm glad you did. Starting out a marriage with a lie can lead to all kinds of trouble, I know."

"It's over, Teresa," Rico murmured gently. "In the past, where it stays."

"I know." She smiled at him, then looked back to Marie. "But I'm pleased that you know. It's so hard to maintain a lie for long."

"Oh, I agree." Marie shrunk into the couch a little.

"Now, back to the wedding," Teresa said and kept sketching out ideas as she spoke again. "Marie, Rico will fly your family in for the ceremony and you and Gianni could stay here on your honeymoon and it would be no problem for us to handle everything, would it, Rico?"

"Teresa," her husband said.

"We do wonderful weddings on Tesoro," Teresa assured Marie. "There is a fabulous little dress shop in the village and I know she would have something you will love—or we could go into St. Thomas for a day of shopping! Wouldn't that be fun? And I will make your wedding cake myself. I would trust no one else with such an important task."

Marie couldn't think of a thing to say and even if she'd been able to, she wasn't sure she would have had a chance to say it. Teresa was running full throttle and there didn't seem to be a way to stop her. Panic began to claw at the base of Marie's throat. *This is not happening....*

"Teresa," her husband said softly, amusement in his voice.

"Come on," Teresa argued, "it's perfect and you know it. What better place than Tesoro for a wedding? It's beautiful, everything's in bloom…"

"Basta," Gianni said, his voice cutting through his sister's monologue. "Enough, Teresa. We're not getting married this week."

Marie sighed in relief. Good. She had been half-afraid

Gianni wouldn't speak up, instead leaving it to her to quash Teresa's plans.

A hotel maid came into the room, carrying a baby bottle. Smiling, she handed it to Teresa, then left again as quietly as she'd come in.

"Give him to me, Rico, and I'll feed him," Teresa said.

"Please," Gianni said, "if she's busy with her son perhaps she'll leave her brother alone."

"I can do both," Teresa assured him as she took her son into her arms and smiled down at the tiny boy.

Marie watched with the tiniest twinge of envy. It was ridiculous, really, to wish for a baby when she almost never went on a date and hadn't even—she cut off that thought fast. Not the time or the place. Instead she looked at the baby, short, chubby arms waving in the air as he waited to be fed. Black hair dusted the infant's head and his eyes were a bright blue just like his father's.

The Kings were a beautiful family and Marie felt more like an outsider every moment. Gianni was lying to them, too, but he actually belonged there. He was Teresa's family. Marie was only a temporary blip on the Coretti family radar. Once she had the Contessa and had returned to New York, these people would forget all about her.

Gianni would go back to his life—a different woman every week. Teresa would still be hoping her brothers would find love and settle down. And that tiny boy Marie watched so closely right now would grow up and never even know she had been here.

As for Marie, she'd be back in New York City. She wasn't naive enough to believe that the board of the Wainwright would reinstate her, so she'd be home and unemployed. She couldn't go back to the police force— being head of security had pretty much ruined her for that. So she'd be scrambling for a job and looking back on a week of designer clothes, tropical islands and sterile white gazillionaire bachelor pads like a hazy dream.

"Explain to me why you don't want to get married this week," Teresa demanded of her brother, kissing her son's forehead before frowning at Gianni. "Your engagement was a whirlwind, as Marie said. Why not your wedding as well?"

"I'm working this week, remember?" Gianni told her with a slow shake of his head. "I'm here for Interpol. And I'm here to see my nephew christened. Isn't that enough for one week?"

It sounded reasonable to Marie.

"I suppose." Disappointment tinged Teresa's voice. "But—"

"No more, Teresa," Gianni told her. "You have a husband and a son now. Bother *them*."

Rico laughed and when his wife looked at him, insulted, he continued to grin then leaned down and kissed her mouth in a firm, brief caress. "He has you there, my love. Now leave him alone."

Shaking her head, Teresa looked to Marie and said, "I wish you luck with my brother. He is a...*testa dura*. Hard-head."

"Very nice," Gianni said and toasted her with his glass of scotch. When the glass was empty, he set it down, reached out and grasped Marie's hand and, holding it, asked, "How many people are attending the jewelry show?"

Rico looked at him thoughtfully. "There are a few dozen designers and jewelers attending, along with some press and a few carefully screened guests."

"Screened?" Marie asked.

Gianni squeezed her hand. "To weed out possible thieves."

"Ah, of course."

"A jewelry show of this magnitude will likely draw the attention of every thief in the world—no matter if they have the skills to pull it off or not." He glanced knowingly at Marie as he said it and she took a quick breath.

He was talking about Jean Luc. Was there a possibility the man might actually show up here? Her heartbeat jumped in sudden anticipation. It came from being a cop, she supposed. But the thought of actually catching Jean Luc and forcing him to hand over the Contessa was so stirring, it was hard to sit still.

Then it occurred to her that if Jean Luc did show up on the island, she would pretty much have to hide because he would recognize her. And if he saw her with Gianni Coretti, he would definitely be suspicious enough to bolt before they could learn anything from him.

"Is there someone in particular I should warn my security about?" Rico asked, apparently picking up on Gianni's subtle message to Marie.

"Jean Luc Baptiste," Gianni said and Teresa's head snapped up to look at her brother.

"Jean Luc?" She wrinkled her nose in distaste. "He wouldn't dare try anything on Tesoro. He's not good enough."

Silently amused, Marie hid a smile. Teresa might not be in the family business, but clearly she still had the sensibilities of a master thief. She was insulted at the very idea of Jean Luc attempting to steal anything from her husband.

"Jean Luc doesn't have the skills," Gianni said, agreeing with his sister. "But he has more than enough ego to make up for that lack. He's so sure of himself and so cocky, it may be enough to convince him he can do it."

"Who is this man?"

Gianni looked at Rico. "He's an arrogant, less-than-skilled thief with delusions of grandeur. He thinks he's much better than he actually is."

Sighing, Marie thought that it was an excellent description of Jean Luc. Of course, he was also handsome, charming and slick enough to sneak past her own internal radar. Humiliating to admit, even to herself, that she had been conned just as any unsuspecting civilian might have been. Knowing that Gianni knew she'd been taken in by a pretty face only added to her private humiliation.

Rico was pacing. "If he's not good enough, why would he risk coming here when he would know that security would be tight enough we would never allow him onto the island?"

Gianni's gaze followed his brother-in-law. "First, he won't use his own name to register—and, he probably won't book a room here at your place, but instead go for the other hotel on the island. Smaller, less security-conscious."

Rico nodded grimly.

Marie was watching Gianni. She could see why Interpol had taken him on in exchange for immunity. He was smart and the knowledge of a master thief would be invaluable.

Rico looked worried. "It still doesn't make sense. If he's not good enough—"

"His arrogance will make this jewelry show irresistible to him." Gianni sat forward on the couch, still holding Marie's hand in his. His thumb caressed her palm and she had to fight to concentrate as he continued speaking.

"He will tell himself that if he can only manage a theft *here,* then his reputation will be made."

"Give me a description of him to hand out to my security team," Rico ordered, obviously convinced.

Teresa spoke up then. "I can describe him for you. We've all known Jean Luc for years."

"Fine then." Gianni stood up and drew Marie to her feet as well. "Now, we're going to our suite to relax and wash up. We'll see you at dinner, all right?"

"Fine, fine," Teresa said, laughing as she waved her free hand at them. "You go ahead. I'm sure your luggage is already in your suite. Rico gave you the same one you had on your last visit, you remember?"

"I do." Still holding Marie's hand, Gianni stepped around the coffee table, bent down and kissed his sister. "Don't worry about Jean Luc ruining anything. Between your husband, his security team and me, he won't get away with anything."

"I know," she said, smiling.

"All right then." Gianni straightened. "See you later."

It wasn't until they'd left the suite that Gianni looked at Marie and said, "That went well."

Eight

They checked in to their suite, unpacked and within fifteen minutes or so, Gianni had Marie out of the hotel room and away from the gigantic bed before he could give in to temptation. The coming week was going to be a hard one, he knew. But no point in torturing himself before he absolutely had to.

"I can't believe this place," Marie said as he steered her around the hotel grounds.

Gianni knew what she was talking about. He'd felt the same way the first time he'd been here about a year before.

Rico had built what was, essentially, a Disneyland for adults. There were infinity pools, private spas and spectacular ocean views from every room. It was a relatively small hotel, to keep it exclusive. There were only a hundred and fifty rooms, not counting the private bungalows tucked away in groves of trees scattered around the grounds.

Rooms were decadent, the service was impeccable and for those who could afford a stay here, King's Castle on Tesoro provided a fantasy come to life.

On Tesoro, the always present trade winds kept insects at a minimum and carried the scent of tropical flowers, flavoring each breath drawn. The ocean was only steps away and farther inland there were forests filled with banyan trees that looked as though they'd been plucked from fairy stories and dropped onto the island for atmosphere.

"It's impressive," Gianni agreed.

Marie stopped walking and looked up at him. Sunlight poured down on her, highlighting the dark fire of her hair until it seemed to burn like a halo around her head. Her green eyes were suddenly serious as she asked, "Did you mean what you said to Rico and Teresa? About Jean Luc, I mean. Do you really think he'll show up here?"

Frowning slightly, his gaze shifted from hers to encompass the pool area. There were lovely women stretched out on rainbow-colored chaises, a couple of people doing laps in the water and servers moving along the tiled walkways, delivering frothy drinks.

This was exactly the kind of atmosphere a man like Jean Luc preferred. He'd only gotten into the jewel-thief world because of his hunger for the good things in life. The Coretti family treated their trade like the job it was. They gave it focus, practice, *respect*. Jean Luc, though, treated it as a game—one he was determined to win. A good thing in some, but in Jean Luc, it made him take what Gianni would see as unnecessary risks. Attempting jobs that he wasn't skilled enough to complete because his own ego demanded it.

"Yes," he said softly, "I do."

"If he comes here, he won't have the Contessa with him."

He looked back at her. "No. He'll leave that at home. No need to carry old trophies when you're looking to steal new ones."

"Right." She nodded and he could see from the gleam in her eyes that her thoughts were racing. "So we'll still have to go to Monaco after the necklace."

"After the conference, yes."

Still nodding, Marie said, "But if we catch him here, that would make things easier all the way around, right?"

"We?" One eyebrow lifted.

She tipped her chin up and met his gaze squarely. "I used to be a cop, remember? And I'm also a security expert. I can help."

"I used to be a thief," he reminded her. "And I think that experience will come in handy this week. Rico's security staff is the best in the world."

"Doesn't mean another set of eyes wouldn't help," she argued. "So, instead of showing me the pools, how about showing me where the jewelry exhibition's going to be?"

He already knew the look she had on her face right now. That fierce blend of determination and stubbornness. And he knew, too, that if he didn't show her the exhibit hall, then she'd simply find it on her own. Better to have him with her.

Pulling his cell phone out of his pocket, he punched in Rico's number. "I'll find out where it's being held."

"Good." Her features brightened and a wide, beautiful smile curved her mouth.

Gianni's insides fisted and his groin tightened painfully. Hunger simmered in his blood and it was a feeling he was becoming all too accustomed to. It wasn't just her beauty that called to him, though—it was so much more. Her self-confidence, her resolve and her sense of purpose all made her almost impossible to resist. *Almost,* because he was doing his damnedest to do just that and he had the distinct impression he was losing the battle.

"Rico," he said when the other man answered. Keeping his gaze locked on Marie, he said, "We'd like to check out the exhibition hall."

"You have some ideas on how to beef up security?"

Gianni laughed a little. "I won't know that until I look around, will I?"

"I'll let Franklin Hicks know you're coming over." Rico took a breath and said, "Franklin's my head of security. Easy to spot. Thirty-five, he stands six foot five and he's got a shaved head and sharp blue eyes."

"Sounds intimidating enough."

"Oh, he is," Rico said with a snort. "Not much gets past him. But I'm sure he'll welcome the input of a man like you."

"Meaning *thief,*" he murmured.

"Meaning one of the best thieves," Rico corrected.

"What's he saying?" Marie demanded.

He held up one hand and listened to Rico as he said, "Teresa gave me a description of this Jean Luc and we're circulating it among the men and posting it in the main security office."

"That's good," Gianni told him. "Can you get that description over to the other hotel on the island as well?"

"Already done," Rico said.

"Description?" Marie asked. "You mean of Jean Luc?"

Shaking her head she muttered, "Haven't you guys ever heard of disguises?"

Gianni snorted, then said, "Yes, Marie is just reminding us that Jean Luc could show up in disguise."

"Perfect," Rico said. "Well, we'll do what we can to spot him anyway."

"We all will."

"Right. Okay then." Rico took a breath and said, "I'll let Franklin know you're coming over."

"Fine. Thanks. We'll see you and Teresa later."

When he hung up, he shrugged and said, "It seems they've cleared out the main dining room to use for the show. We can go over now to check it out. Rico's calling his man to tell them we're coming."

Her smile widened. "That's great. Let's go."

Gianni took her hand and headed for the front of the hotel. What other woman in the world would choose to walk a security perimeter around a dining room instead of taking a tour of a luxury resort? One, he told himself, that was beginning to be way too important to him.

The dining room had been transformed.

Gianni remembered it as an elegant space with soft lighting, windows affording a magnificent view of the ocean and servers who were as inconspicuous as they were efficient. There were usually dozens of small, round tables, each displaying a small vase of tropical flowers dotting the space.

Today, though, the dining room boasted several long, antique tables, covered in red velvet that lent the atmosphere of old-world opulence. The lighting was soft, making the golden bamboo floors seem to glow. There were chairs set up behind privacy screens, where designers could take patrons who wanted a little one-on-one time with the gems.

At the head of the room, there was a conversation area set up with bloodred sofas and chairs clustered around glass and bamboo tables, where designers and clients could talk comfortably. The beauty the hotel was known for was on display, from the gleaming polish on the floor to the brass wall sconces and the wide, uninterrupted view of the ocean through the glass wall.

"Are the glass walls and windows wired, do you think?"

He glanced at Marie. "That's a good question. I don't know for sure, but with Rico, I'm guessing the answer is yes. He leaves very little to chance."

And Gianni could see that security was definitely heightened as there were tiny, discreet cameras everywhere. It only took him a moment to count at least twelve, posted about the room, each providing different angles. Marie was as aware as he.

"I count twelve eyes out in the open," she said, her gaze narrowed as she took another longer, slower look.

"Agreed." Gianni nodded toward the far corner. "And no doubt there are many more that are less obvious. For instance, I think I see a hidden camera in that urn of hibiscus blooms."

"Good one." She smiled and said, "And the one peeking out from behind the framed painting on the south wall."

Enjoying himself, he grinned down at her. He'd never met a woman like her. "Can you see a spot they've missed?"

"Hard to tell unless you can be in the security office and see the camera feeds," she mused thoughtfully. Turning in a slow circle, she scanned the room. "It's always difficult to line up cameras so that the angles they cover overlap without leaving blind spots. But I'm guessing they haven't missed much."

"Probably not," Gianni agreed. "But there are always holes. No security is perfect. As you said, camera angles can only spread so far and a good thief doesn't need much of an opening."

"True." She looked up at him. "You were a good thief, right?"

He sent her a quick smile. "Master jewel thief."

"Right." Her own smile was just a flash. "So, Master Jewel Thief, if you were going to hit this place, how would you do it?"

"Ahh." He sighed to himself at the thought. It wouldn't be the first time he would use his imagination to commit a heist. He liked to think of it as a mental exercise. Keeping his skill set sharp even though he wasn't using those skills anymore. He had to stay on top of intercepting would-be thieves if he wanted to remain useful to Interpol—and besides, he admitted silently, it was fun. Yes, he was on the straight-and-narrow path now, but he could dream.

And when he dreamed it was of things like this. A scenario where the owner had taken all precautions. Where the reward for pulling off the job would be immeasurable. And where it would take all of his skill to complete the task and not get caught.

A familiar buzz of adrenaline pumped through his system as he turned his imagination loose. He looked at the glass wall and the tables closest to it. At the windows on either end of the long dining hall and at the ceiling fifteen feet overhead. There was always a way. Air-conditioning ducts, he thought as his gaze slid over them, though crawling through those enclosed spaces was a hideous job. Enclosed spaces felt too much like prison for Gianni. Or he could come in through the skylight that right now showcased a brilliant blue sky.

"So many possibilities," he murmured.

"You miss it."

He looked at her, surprised that she'd caught him. Or maybe not. Marie O'Hara seemed to pick up on things that most others didn't—or wouldn't. Letting go of the imaginary plan for robbing Rico's hotel, he focused instead on how he felt about giving up the life he'd always known.

"I suppose I do," he mused. "The thrill of outwitting security systems. The challenge of working out just the right plan of attack. Slipping into a home or business and getting out again without being noticed. Walking along a rooftop when the night is so black you can't see your own hand in front of your face and you have to trust your instincts to keep from killing yourself." He smiled fondly. "It's a world not many people will ever know."

"You make it sound as though it was just about the planning and the job itself," she said softly and he watched as she pushed a long strand of dark red hair behind her ear. "So it wasn't the stealing that was the draw for you? I mean, the things you stole."

His lips quirked as that strand of hair slipped free again and he reached out to tuck it behind her ear for her, letting his fingertips slide across her skin in a brief caress. That slight touch burned his skin as if he'd touched a live wire—and maybe he had. "I would be lying if I said that and I think you know it."

She nodded, and kept quiet, waiting for him to continue.

He'd never tried to explain what he did before. Never tried to make sense of it all to a civilian. But then, Marie wasn't entirely a civilian, either, was she? She knew as much about crime as he did—only from a different perspective. And he suddenly found that he *wanted* her to understand it from his point of view.

"A thief doesn't break into guarded places simply for the pleasure of being able to do it. There must be a reward at the end of the job, of course." He picked up her left hand, and rubbed his thumb over the ring she wore. One of his trophies from a successful job. "I'm not really sure how to explain to you what it's like, Marie. No one can really *know* it unless they've lived it."

"Try," she whispered, closing her fingers around his.

Staring into her beautiful summer green eyes, he said softly, "This ring, for example. Armed only with a penlight, I opened the safe—"

"You're a safecracker, too?" she asked, a tiny hint of a smile curving her mouth.

"All Corettis are taught the tricks of our trade from an early age," he told her. "Lock-picking, safecracking, picking pockets—"

"Really?"

"Have to have light and clever fingers if you want to live life as a thief and not a prisoner." He shrugged off his observation and went back into his story. "With everyone downstairs at the party, the second floor of the home was empty and the study where the safe was located was breathlessly still. Black as pitch in there but for slivers of moonlight peeking in and out of the clouds. I was hurrying because it's always best not to waste time."

"I can imagine," she said wryly.

He grinned. "Can't go too fast or you get sloppy. Can't go too slow or you get caught. It's a fine line. Anyway, I opened the safe, reached inside and pulled out a black velvet bag. I knew what I would find inside it, Paulo and I had scoped the place out for months. We knew where the jewels were kept, which jewels were in which safe...."

"There was more than one?"

"Always. But even knowing what I would find, I had to look." Shrugging, he added, "Paulo and I had put a lot of effort into that job, I wanted to see the treasure at the end of the rainbow. I poured the contents into my palm and a moonbeam hit the diamonds and brought them to life."

She was quiet now, watching him, their gazes locked as he reminisced and shared a piece of himself that he'd shared with no one else.

"There was a choker necklace with seventy-seven diamonds set in platinum and this ring," he said, rubbing her finger again gently. "Locked away in the darkness, as if they had been sentenced to oblivion. When they slid from the bag and the moonlight shone on them it was as if they sighed and thanked me for rescuing them. Diamonds are meant to shine, to be in the light, to be worn and admired and envied." His smile deepened as he said, "When I watched the moonlight on those stones, it was like magic. Like seeing something cold and forgotten and...dead, burst into life again."

She glanced down to where his thumb still moved across the surface of the ring she wore. "And so you kept the ring to remind you of that moment."

"I did, yes," he said, then added with a grin, "and to give to my lovely fiancée, of course."

Her lips moved as if she were trying to keep from smiling and he thought that perhaps her strict black-and-white outlook was beginning to gray just a little. Why did he find that so damn sexy?

"And the necklace?" she asked.

"Ah…" He released her hand and said, "That, Paulo and I sold for our first fortune."

"You're not sorry at all, are you?"

"For being a thief?" he asked and when he saw that was what she meant, he said, "No. I was very good at what I did. I worked at it for years and I never hurt anyone—just their insurance companies." His lips curved. "I won't be sorry for who I am, who I come from or the choices made. What would be the point? The past is done, being sorry changes nothing."

"But—"

"Don't mistake my newfound path for shame at my past." Gianni cupped the back of her neck in his palm and leaned into her. "I am a Coretti and I will never be ashamed of my family or my heritage. How I choose to live my life now has nothing to do with that past, beyond a brief moment of epiphany that sent me in a new direction. I am, at my heart, a thief, Marie."

She shook her head and speared his gaze with hers. "You're not, Gianni. At your heart, you're so much more."

"Don't fool yourself," he warned, though he loved the warmth he read in her eyes. She was looking at him now and seeing the man—not the thief—and he enjoyed it. He wanted her to see him as more than his profession. But he couldn't let her believe that the thief no longer existed inside the man. Because he did. Gianni would always feel that tug of interest, of *want,* when he saw diamonds.

When he saw the opportunity for a job that appealed to him. That desire would always be a part of him.

"Don't believe I'm more than what you see," he said softly. "I am the man whose apartment you broke in to. The one you despised."

"I didn't despise you—"

One eyebrow lifted at that statement. He cupped her cheek in the palm of his hand. "You did. And that's all right. Probably better that you focus on that feeling. It will help you remember that this engagement between us is nothing more than the charade we agreed on."

She covered his hand with her own. "I'm not the one having trouble remembering that, Gianni."

The truth of that statement startled him enough that he released her and took a healthy step backward. He was in trouble. He had forgotten, at least temporarily, how this thing between them had started and just why exactly they were there, on Tesoro. She was his blackmailer, nothing more. She held his family's safety in her hands and instead of keeping that thought firmly in mind, he was spending far too much time thinking about getting her into bed. About getting his hands on her.

"Mr. Coretti?"

Grateful for the interruption, he looked up to see a tall man with a shaven head and sharp blue eyes approaching. No doubt Rico's head of security and Gianni had to give his brother-in-law credit. As a professional thief, Gianni could recognize the danger in this man. He would be a formidable enemy.

"Yes. Franklin Hicks?"

"That's me," the man said with a nod. Looking to Marie, he said, "Ms. O'Hara. Mr. King asked that I show the two of you the security system for the upcoming show and answer any questions you might have."

Gianni didn't much care for the way the bald giant was scrutinizing Marie. There was a gleam in his eye that was pure male appreciation and it made Gianni want to throw her behind him and protect her from the other man's gaze.

"Thank you." Marie glanced at Gianni then turned her attention back to the other man. "We'd appreciate that."

As Hicks led the way across the showroom floor, Gianni brought up the rear behind the other two. And, of course, whether he wanted to admit it or not, his gaze dropped to the curve of Marie's behind. Didn't seem to matter how often he told himself to keep his mind on the job at hand. Clearly, his body was more interested in other things.

"The bed's more than wide enough for us both." Gianni sprawled across the mattress and opened his arms as if to welcome her.

Marie took a deep breath and locked her knees so she couldn't give in to temptation even if she wanted to. Which she didn't. Really. It was just that she hadn't had any sleep in days. That's why the bed looked so good. It wasn't because of the gorgeous man lying across it.

Glancing around the sumptuous room, Marie took it all in and tried to look casual. She felt Gianni's eyes on her and deliberately avoided looking back at him. Instead, she noted the open French doors leading to a patio that overlooked an awe-inspiring ocean view. The bamboo floor shone in the sunlight and was softened by rugs in jewel tones scattered around the room. There was a sitting area in front of a gas fireplace and a silver bucket holding champagne on a small table between the matching chairs. Beside the glass wall, a peach-colored chaise offered a spot to curl up and watch the ocean. The walls were cream-colored, but enlivened by bright, tropical paintings and filmy curtains that waved in the ever-present wind like fluttering spirits.

There was a huge attached bath with a tub big enough to hold four people comfortably and a shower area that was open to the room and boasted six jets. But Marie had to admit that the star of the show was the bed.

It was gigantic, covered in a duvet of sea-foam green and stacked with pillows against the honey-colored wood headboard. But it was the man on top of it that looked irresistible. Gianni's dark hair looked as black as midnight against the stark white of the pillows. His chest was broad, his grin enticing, and she was having a very hard time resisting the urge to toss herself across that chest.

"We're not sharing that bed," she said firmly and wondered if she were trying to convince him or herself.

"Up to you," he said and his Italian accent became thicker, more alluring. "But I don't think you'll be very comfortable on that chaise."

Marie blinked at him. "If you were a gentleman, you'd offer to sleep on the chaise."

"Ah, but I'm not a gentleman, am I?" He tucked his arms behind his head and snuggled into the pillows at his back. "I'm a thief."

"So you're going to let me sleep on that?" she asked.

"I've invited you to share my bed," he pointed out.

Marie gritted her teeth. He was enjoying this. And why shouldn't he? Gianni would be sleeping very well on a wide, spectacular bed and she would be curled up on one side trying not to roll off a chaise that looked a lot more narrow all of a sudden.

"We are engaged after all," he said softly, his voice a tempting purr.

That twist of hot and achy need throbbed inside her again, and Marie took a deep breath to steady herself. It didn't really help, but it was all she had.

"You're the one who warned me not to forget that this was all a charade, Gianni," she said.

His features tightened, eyes narrowed and the sexy smile faded away. "You're right. I did. Then by all means, Marie. Keep your distance. Because," he added, gaze locked on hers, "if you share this bed with me, it won't be for sleeping, I promise you."

Two days later, Marie lazed in the sun and felt the lovely trade winds caressing her skin as the sunlight warmed her through. The view of the ocean soothed her twisted nerves and the privacy was like a balm. Being here at Teresa and Rico's private pool atop the hotel was a gift. Here, she could relax her guard—somewhat. She still had to maintain her cover as Gianni's fiancée in front of Teresa, of course. But at least she was getting a break from the constant barrage of sensations she had to fight against when she was with Gianni.

She hadn't had a decent night's sleep since she'd begun this whole adventure. And the situation had only gotten more difficult since they'd arrived on Tesoro. Sharing that opulent, sensual suite with him was shredding what was left of Marie's self-control.

Gianni's promise kept resonating in her mind…. *It won't be for sleeping.* Her mind had conjured all sorts of delicious scenarios that kept her awake and aching all night—while *he* seemed to be sleeping just fine! She listened to his deep, even breathing and wanted to shriek in frustration. Instead, she lay on that narrow, uncomfortable chaise and counted all the ways in which it would be a bad idea to have sex with Gianni.

Sadly, though, those very logical reasons were disappearing into a flood of want that kept rising inside her. She was so tempted to surrender, it was tearing her in two to keep from joining him on the bed, giving in to what she wanted and finally easing the torment that was with her every waking minute.

Shaking her head, she told herself to be strong. She could do this. Tonight was the first event for the jewelry show. Designers and customers would be meeting in the showroom for cocktails and music at the grand opening. In three days, she'd attend the baby's christening and then once the jewelry show ended, she and Gianni would leave for Monaco to find Jean Luc and the Contessa. Then this would all be over. She could go back to her staid, boring life and forget all about this blip on her own personal radar.

"What's really going on between you and Gianni?"

Marie jolted and looked over at Teresa. Sitting poolside, they were sharing snacks and a really amazing sparkling peach drink that Marie suddenly wished had a lot of vodka in it. The baby was sleeping inside and it was just she and Teresa here on the patio.

"What do you mean?"

Teresa laughed shortly and tipped her sunglasses down to peer at her. "Oh, come on, Marie. I know something's up. I've never seen Gianni so on edge. I mean, for a man in love he looks like a tortured soul around you."

"He does?"

Teresa smiled gently. "And so do you. So what's going on?"

Good question, she thought. It made her feel better to think that Gianni wasn't quite as cool and calm as she had believed him to be. And knowing Teresa was suspicious suddenly took the pressure of keeping up the pretense off her shoulders. Maybe she shouldn't say anything, but the opportunity to actually talk to someone about all of this made it impossible to resist.

Marie thought about it for another ten whole seconds and then she made her decision and started talking. She only half noticed the expressions chasing themselves across Teresa's features while she talked. They ranged from shock to fear to amusement and back again, but Marie kept talking. It was such a relief to say it all out loud, she hadn't really considered how the whole blackmail thing would sound to the daughter of the man Marie was threatening. When she finally wound down, she waited for Teresa's reaction. She didn't wait long.

"You have evidence against my father?"

Flushing, Marie admitted, "Yes." She swung her legs off the chaise and faced the other woman. "I do. But I don't want to use it."

Hearing that said out loud, Marie could admit to herself that it was true. She didn't want to hurt the Coretti family. Didn't want to turn an old man into the police so that he lived the rest of his life in a prison cell. She wasn't a cop anymore—she didn't *owe* it to society. But at the same time, she wanted and needed to be able to return the necklace to Abigail Wainwright. For her own sense of rightness. Justice.

"But you blackmailed Gianni with it?"

"I didn't really have a choice, Teresa. He never would

have helped me catch Jean Luc if I didn't have some leverage."

"Yes, I understand that." Teresa blew out a breath. "But Papa…"

Marie tried to explain. "I know how it sounds. But the theft in New York? It was my fault. I let Jean Luc charm me into relaxing my guard and he used the opportunity to steal from a lovely old woman who didn't deserve to have her home invaded and her property stolen."

Teresa frowned. "No, she didn't. And I even understand how Jean Luc could charm you if you didn't really know the man." Frowning, she sat up, too, and faced Marie. "I can't say that I am thrilled with the fact that you're threatening my father, but I understand the sense of honor that's driving you."

"Thank you," Marie said, relieved now not only to have the truth out, but to also have Teresa appreciate just what a spot she'd been in to have sunk to blackmail in the first place. She really liked these people. Had felt envy for the life Teresa had—oh, not the money so much, but the doting husband and adorable baby. For having her place in the world defined and the people she loved with her.

Marie hadn't had that in a long time and seeing it play out before her eyes was enough to make her long for the same things.

"I believe," Teresa said, "that you don't really want to put Papa in jail, either, but only used what you had to get what you needed."

"Exactly. And really, the more I learn about Gianni and the rest of you, the less interested I am in seeing your father put behind bars. But there's no stopping now.

I have to go through with this and if I gave the evidence to Gianni, why would he help me?"

"You might be surprised," Teresa said thoughtfully. Then she asked, "But what happens when you find Jean Luc? When you retrieve the stolen property? What happens between you and Gianni then?"

"We go back to our lives," Marie said softly.

"That easily?" Teresa shook her head, reached out and took one of Marie's hands in hers. "I don't think so. However this started, there is more between the two of you now than either of you wish to acknowledge."

"You're wrong," Marie insisted, though that curl of heat and desire and need throbbed deep inside just as relentlessly as it had for the last several days.

"I disagree. Let me tell you a story," Teresa said, keeping Marie's hand in hers. "It is about Rico and me and mistakes made."

While Teresa talked, Marie listened and was amazed that Rico and Teresa had been able to work things out and build such a strong marriage and family now. Their lives had begun on a lie and somehow, they'd found a way past it.

"I know what it is to hold honor so high you lose sight of everything else that is equally important," Teresa told her. "To protect my father and brothers, I gave up Rico and for five years, I missed him, died every day without him. And when finally we came together again it was my family's honor that almost kept us apart once more." She squeezed Marie's hand.

"The difference was, you and Rico loved each other in spite of everything," Marie said.

"And you love my brother."

"What?" Marie tugged her hand free of Teresa's grip,

shook her head and blindly grabbed for her frothy, girlie drink that so needed a shot or two of vodka. Teresa's words slapped at her, insisting they be recognized, but she couldn't do it. Couldn't look that closely at what she'd been feeling for days.

She and Gianni didn't have a real relationship. What they had was a charade that was quickly hurtling toward its conclusion. So feeling *anything* would be a huge mistake.

"You're wrong. I hardly know Gianni. I certainly don't love him."

"You think I don't recognize the signs?" Teresa smiled at her in sympathy. "You watch him whenever he comes into a room. You tremble when he touches you and he infuriates you so easily, there must be love at the heart of it. The only people who can push us over the edge so completely are those we care about."

"Care is one thing," Marie grabbed onto the word *care* like a life raft in a churning sea. Of course she cared about Gianni. He was warm and kind and funny along with being irritating. And of course she *wanted* him. A woman would have to be dead for a year to not want him. "Love is another."

Love didn't come on in a flash of heat. It grew slowly, quietly, with two people learning about each other, finding places in each other's lives. There had to be common interests, friendship as well as attraction. There had to be…more.

"This isn't about love, Teresa," she argued, determined to keep her mind focused. "Lust, maybe, but not love."

The other woman just smiled again and Marie thought that all of the Corettis could be a little irritating.

"I know my brother," Teresa said. "He is protective

of our family. Even with the threat you posed, he would never have brought you here, to the island, if he didn't feel—"

"There you are!" Gianni's voice cut off Teresa before she could finish her sentence.

Which left Marie internally shrieking *What? If he didn't feel what?*

Rico was right behind Gianni and the two men converged on them with a few hurried strides. Gianni looked down at Marie and she felt the heat in his gaze as he looked her up and down and then back up again. She was wearing a new bikini, purchased in London, and she knew the lime-green scraps of fabric looked pretty good on her. Judging by Gianni's expression now, maybe it looked even better than pretty good.

He stared at her for a couple more seconds, until Teresa chuckled. The sound shook him out of the trance he seemed to be in. Meeting Marie's eyes he said simply, "We found Jean Luc. He's here. On the island."

Nine

A half hour later, they were in their suite. Gianni stared down Marie and waited for her to back off from her ridiculous argument. But she wouldn't and he should have expected it. The woman had been absolutely uncooperative since the moment he'd caught her searching his bedroom. Why did he enjoy it so much?

"I should be there. I can help you look for Jean Luc."

He shoved one hand through his hair and wished to hell she would put on a robe or something. It was damned hard to concentrate on an argument when distracted by the luscious curves so openly displayed by that tiny, lime-green bikini.

His body was tight and hard, and looking at her had his blood pumping and his heart racing. At the moment, he couldn't care less about Jean Luc Baptiste and in fact would have happily cursed the man to the bottom of

the ocean. But since he couldn't do that, he was forced
to deal with the fact that Jean Luc was here, on Tesoro,
and they had to protect the jewelry show from his all-too
sticky fingers. And, if possible, keep him from seeing
Marie here. Jean Luc wasn't the most brilliant thief on
the planet, but he was smart enough to realize that she
didn't belong here.

Gianni scrubbed both hands across his face. "Jean
Luc's staying in the older hotel on the island. The one
owned by Rico's cousin Sean's wife's grandfather."

She shook her head as if confused.

"Yes, I know. Convoluted. Anyway, he's staying there,
but he's been here at Rico's place, too. Security's spotted him on the grounds and we're going to try to catch
him tonight."

"If he hasn't stolen anything yet, how can you capture him?"

He huffed out a breath. "It's like they do at casinos
when they see a known thief. He hasn't done anything
in *their* place yet, but his reputation is enough to see him
escorted out."

"Fine. They escort him out and off the island, I guess."

"Exactly." He nodded briefly. "It's a privately owned
island, they can throw him off if they wish."

"But first you have to catch him and I can help with
that," she argued, planting both fists at her hips. "I'm
another set of eyes."

She was far more than that, Gianni thought, trying
to keep his mind on the problem at hand rather than the
body he wanted to hold. He was caught in a trap of his
own making. This whole thing had been his idea. The
pretense of an engagement. Staying in close quarters,
where the very thought of her sleeping on a chaise only

a few feet from his bed was making him a little more insane every day.

She sighed and he hungered. She laughed and he needed. She kissed him and set fire to all of the dark, empty corners inside him. Dark corners that had been with him so long, he'd ceased even being aware of them years ago. But Marie had made him notice them again. Made him realize that his life hadn't been as full as he'd told himself. He was too much alone. Too insular, even from the family he loved.

But now there was her. And he didn't know what the hell to do about it. Pushing back the racing thoughts careening through his mind, he snapped.

"And if he sees you first? Then what?" Gianni threw his hands high. "Even Jean Luc isn't stupid enough to believe that your being here on the eve of an exclusive jewelry show is a coincidence."

She muttered something dark under her breath then said aloud, "Why shouldn't I be here?"

Gianni snorted. "And did your security job pay well enough that you could afford a vacation on Tesoro?"

Her mouth twisted. "No, but for all he knows I could have family money. What does it matter if he sees me?"

"Thieves are superstitious," he told her, grasping at straws to keep her away from Jean Luc. He didn't need the thief panicking at the sight of her. "Bad thieves are even more so. If Jean Luc sees you here, he'll bolt—he'll run without making a play for the jewels. And if he does that," he added, hoping this would be enough to convince her, "he might even close down his place in Monaco and disappear. Then how will we get your necklace back?"

Not that he really believed that. If anything, Jean Luc would run straight to his home on Monaco's coast and probably hole up until the next tempting job came up. But Marie didn't know that.

Behind her, the French doors were open, allowing the wind and sun to slide into the room. She was backlit and there was a nimbus of golden light along every line of her body. If he were a fanciful man he would have thought she looked like something that stepped out of a dream world.

Since he was more pragmatic than that, Gianni only thought that she was the stuff dreams were made of. Her skin was smooth and silky; her hair tumbled around her face in a cluster of loose curls and waves. Everything about her was tempting. Even the flash of anger in her eyes and the defiant tilt of her chin.

She gritted her teeth. Jaw tight, she folded her arms across her chest and unconsciously lifted her breasts so high they threatened to spill from behind the small triangles of fabric. His mouth watered, his hands itched to touch her, and so he folded his hands into fists at his sides to keep from giving in to that urge.

"Fine. You win this one. I won't go with you to the jewelry show."

"Good." Battle won.

"But make sure you talk to Rico about the possibility of blind spots in the camera angles," she added.

"We already discussed that with Franklin Hicks the other day, remember?"

"Right." She took a breath and blew it out on a long sigh of frustration. "So now I get to play damsel in distress or something is that it? Stay tucked away while the big strong men take care of everything?"

"Thank you very much. I do work out."

She just stared at him for a long minute and then laughed helplessly. "You're unbelievable."

"So I've been told. Repeatedly."

Shaking her hair back from her face, she stomped furiously across the room and into the adjoining bath. When she came back out into the main room, she was wearing a thick, white terry-cloth robe provided by the hotel. She tied the belt around her waist and Gianni wanted to both thank her and beg her to take it off again.

The woman was turning his brain to jelly.

"I really hate this."

"I know," he said. "But look at it this way. If we catch Jean Luc, we can force him to give you the necklace."

"How?"

"I can be very persuasive," he assured her. "Catching Jean Luc snooping around an exclusive jewelry exhibition will not be good for him. The threat of alerting Interpol to his presence could be enough to get him to see things our way."

"Could be," she repeated.

"Sì," he murmured, then added, "Jean Luc has not been as careful in his past as the Coretti family. He has a record and won't want the police talking to him." Now that Marie was wearing a robe, his brain could work again and now that they had the issue of her keeping a distance from Jean Luc settled, there was something else he wanted to know. "When Rico and I joined you and my sister on the patio, I got the impression that we had interrupted something."

"No," she said, turning away to walk out onto the terrace.

Gianni didn't believe her. He followed, enjoying the heat of the sun and the cool kiss of the wind, not to mention the sight of Marie, standing against the iron railing while that wind teased her hair into a dark halo about her head.

"You were right, you know," he said.

She looked at him. "About what?"

"When we first met, you told me you weren't a very good liar. You're not." He joined her at the rail. "What were you and Teresa talking about?"

"Truths," she said, tipping her head up to look at him. "I told her the truth. That we're not engaged—"

She surprised him. Again. He hadn't thought she would admit anything for fear of putting herself in a poor light. Yet perhaps he should have expected that her bone-deep honesty would win out in the end. "You told her that you blackmailed me."

"Yes." Sighing, Marie added, "Your sister's so nice I felt hideous lying to her."

He shook his head. "I understand. But, Teresa will tell Paulo and our father."

"So what?" she asked, shrugging as if she were dropping a heavy weight off her shoulders. "It doesn't matter now, does it? I'll still be your cover for Interpol—though how it's going to work if you don't let me attend the show I don't know—"

"Once we catch Jean Luc that will change."

"*If* you catch Jean Luc."

"Leave Jean Luc to me. I know how he thinks." Then he said, "You shouldn't have told Teresa. I didn't want the family to know that there was a threat against Papa."

"Your sister is pretty relentless," Marie said, slumping a little against the railing in front of her. "She knew something was wrong and she wouldn't let it go."

He shifted his gaze from her to the wide sweep of the

ocean stretching out in front of them. Sailboats skimmed the surface of the water and tanned bodies, stretched out on towels, littered the sand.

"Truth," he muttered, more to himself than to her. "It's overrated."

She laughed a little. "Figures a thief would think so."

He looked at her and waited for her to meet his gaze before whispering, "Ex-thief."

"Right," she said, a smile curving her mouth. "I keep forgetting." Turning, she braced one hip against the railing. "Well, here's another truth. Since your family knows about us, we don't have to share this suite. We can have separate rooms."

"Oh, didn't I tell you?" He reached out and pushed at the edge of her robe, sliding it over her shoulder until the top of her breast was bared. She went absolutely still. He slid his fingertips across the flesh exposed, making her shiver while at the same time, sending a shaft of blazing heat to his groin. "The hotel is booked solid. There are no more rooms."

She sucked in a breath and held it.

"Looks as though we're stuck with each other."

"For now," she said.

"Now is all that matters." He moved in on her, and to please himself—and yes, maybe heighten the torture holding him in its grip—he bent his head and kissed her.

He hadn't meant it to be more than a brief meeting of lips. But the moment his mouth claimed hers, it became more. So much more. Heat and light flashed through him and had him grabbing hold of her, pulling her in close and tight until her breasts were flush against his chest and he would have sworn he could feel her heartbeat pounding in time with his.

She moved into him, wrapping her arms around his neck and clinging to him as she kissed him back, her tongue tangling with his. He tasted her breath and sensed her need mounting with his and that fed the flames threatening to engulf him.

There on the terrace, their bodies locked together, Gianni took everything she was willing to give and silently asked for more. He had the feeling that no matter how close he held her it would never be close enough. No matter how deep the kiss, he would want deeper. His body ached for hers. His mind was a rush of thought and color and sensation and if he didn't pull away now, he told himself wildly, he never would be able to.

With that thought uppermost in his mind, Gianni broke the kiss that was killing him and rested his forehead against hers until he had his breathing back under control.

"Well, then," she whispered after a long moment, "I guess there's a lot to be said for *now*."

"Papa's not going to jail." Gianni held his cell phone in one tight fist and scowled at the night as his brother shouted into his ear.

For the last three hours, he had mingled with the crowd celebrating the opening of the jewelry exhibition. Gianni and Rico's security force had become a part of that crowd, though separate. He had watched, listened, slipped into and out of shadows, all the while watching for possible problems as well as for Jean Luc Baptiste. He'd found nothing. If Jean Luc were here tonight, he had become a master of disguise in the last year.

Gianni felt the same tension that used to be his constant companion when on a job. But this tension vibrated at another level. The same and yet different. And as if he weren't tense enough already, this conversation with his brother would put the finishing touches on it.

"Teresa told me everything," Paulo repeated and Gianni rolled his eyes. He'd known this would happen. As soon as Marie admitted confessing all to his sister, Gianni had been half expecting this phone call. It was only a wonder it had taken Paulo so long. Gianni walked along the edge of the terrace, with the showroom behind him. He wasn't sorry to leave the crush of elegant people even if it meant dealing with his younger brother.

"She's blackmailing you!" Paulo's voice got louder and Gianni pulled the phone from his ear. "She holds evidence against our father and you're *sleeping* with her?"

"I'm not—" Gianni stopped himself and took a breath. Damned if he would admit that he hadn't yet gotten Marie into bed. "It's none of your business, brother, who I sleep with."

"It is when thinking with your *cazzo* threatens the family."

Gianni flushed with fury. Eyes wild, he turned away from the dazzling showroom behind him and focused on the black ocean shot with moonlight. He studied each of those shards of light rippling on the water in order to focus the anger churning inside him.

Thankfully, he was alone on the stone terrace, with everyone else hovering around display tables and talking to the designers. Champagne was flowing like a river and Gianni knew that no one inside was going to miss him.

"You think I would risk our father's safety?" Gianni demanded in a strained hush to avoid being overheard by anyone who might choose to step through the French doors. "I'm the one trying to get you and Papa to give up thieving so you can avoid jail altogether."

"Changing the subject, Gianni?"

"Not changing, reminding you of who is the older brother," he snapped. "You don't lecture me, Paulo, on what I do for our family."

There was a long, silent moment and Gianni could almost see Paulo calming down. Yes, the man had a hot temper and a short fuse but that anger never lasted long, either.

"Fine. But Papa and I will be there in a day or so and I want to meet this woman."

Gianni's gaze focused on the beach. Moonlight was bright enough to make out the figure of a lone woman walking along the shoreline. His gaze narrowed on the woman and it only took him a second or two to recognize Marie.

She was supposed to stay in the suite. Did the woman never listen to him?

"You will meet her," Gianni said. "And you will be pleasant or I will not be happy."

"I'm *always* pleasant!" Paulo sounded outraged.

Gianni snorted. "Like now, you mean? You shout and bellow and I'm to take that as 'pleasant'?"

"We're Italian, Gianni," his brother said. "Shouting is expected."

Another lone figure walked the sand, Gianni noticed. A man. And he was headed right toward Marie. She was staring out to sea and not aware of the man's approach. In his head, Gianni knew that she was safe here on Tesoro. Yet, his heart worried. And his senses were suddenly going on alert. Frowning, Gianni watched as the man continued to get nearer to her. Something about him bothered Gianni enough that he said, "*Ciao,* Paulo," and shut his phone off before dropping it into his pants pocket.

It was probably nothing. Yet before he even thought about it, he had vaulted over the railing and hit the sand at a run.

Marie hated being shut out of what was happening at the showroom. She had experience, sharp eyes and skills that could have been of help. Instead, she'd been closed up in her room like a child while the adults took care of the situation. There was too much cop in her to risk ruining an operation by showing up where she wasn't expected, so she didn't go to the jewelry show even though it was killing her not to.

But at the same time, she refused to be locked away, either. She was going stir-crazy in the hotel suite, wondering what was happening, so finally she'd decided to go down to the beach. As long as she stayed clear of the showroom, it shouldn't be a problem. After all, Jean Luc wasn't here to steal grains of sand, now was he?

But to be honest, she admitted, Jean Luc wasn't the one taking up a lot of her thoughts. It was Gianni. She stopped at the water's edge and let the incoming tide slide across her toes in a warm, silky caress before rushing back to the sea.

That kiss. What was she supposed to make of it?

He touched her and she burned, he kissed her and she went completely up in flames. She thought maybe Teresa was right. Maybe he did care for her and she was willing to admit that yes, she cared for him, too. But it wasn't real, was it? It couldn't be. It was too far away from normalcy for Marie to think there was anything beyond this moment in time for she and Gianni.

She hadn't even known him a week, yet it felt as though she'd known him forever. How was that even possible? How could she feel so much for a man who hadn't been a part of her life two weeks before? And how could she pretend to believe that any of it meant anything? This wasn't real life. This wasn't her world.

She was standing in a playground for the rich and famous, daydreaming about a jewel thief turned good guy. How could *any* of it be real?

"I knew it was you."

Her breath caught and she whirled around at the sound of that familiar voice. Moonlight splashed across the man's features and just for a moment, Marie wondered how she had ever thought him to be handsome. His blond hair was too thin, too long, his blue eyes too bland and his jaw and chin looked weak. He wasn't even as tall as she remembered. "Hello, Jean Luc."

Strolling toward her as if he were lord of the beach, he swept her up and down. "Why are you so far from home, Marie? And why are you here with Gianni Coretti?"

She took a breath, planning to lie, but he must have seen it because he shook his head. "Don't bother. I saw the two of you together yesterday."

Well, then staying in her room would have been pointless even if she had actually done it, Marie reasoned.

"Why, Marie?" he demanded, his voice low, his eyes narrowed on her as he came closer. His French accent seemed thicker somehow when he continued. "Why are you here? With him?"

Marie subtly shifted her feet in the sand, taking up a defensive posture—just in case. She was alone down here on the beach and if Jean Luc tried anything, she was going to be ready for it. Though the man had never struck her as dangerous. Just a miserable, lying, cheating thief.

"Did you use him to look for me?" A slow smile curved his mouth. "I'm flattered. Is it because we never had sex? Do you regret that, Marie?" He reached for her. "I regretted it, too. But we can fix that tonight."

Before she could tell him *no* he grabbed her and yanked her in for a kiss. Marie pulled her right arm back, made a fist and prepared to drop him like a sack of rocks.

Then he was gone.

Marie staggered unsteadily, surprised and not sure what was happening. She heard the fight before she saw it. Fists hitting flesh. Someone crashing to the sand. A moan of pain and then Gianni was there in front of her, grabbing her up and pulling her in tightly to him. "Are you all right?"

"I'm fine." She locked her arms around his neck and held on. She could have handled Jean Luc on her own, but having Gianni ride in on his metaphorical white charger had been…nice. Romantic. And feeling the frenzied strength in his arms as he held her now only made that moment even more deeply felt.

She tucked her face into the curve of his neck and shoulder and breathed deep, drawing the scent that was purely him deep into her lungs. How he'd known to come to her she didn't know. But she was glad he was here and when he kissed her hungrily, Marie kissed him back, knowing that the *now* they were experiencing was going to change everything.

Gianni held her as tightly as he could and still wanted her closer. When he'd rushed to the beach he hadn't really thought Marie was in danger. He'd been prepared to lecture her about leaving the suite when they'd agreed that she would stay hidden away. But then he saw Jean Luc grabbing her, touching her, attempting to kiss her—and the world was lost in a wash of red.

He'd never been so angry in his life. Hadn't really believed he could feel such wild passion and rage. But the thought of another man's hands on Marie had pushed Gianni over the edge.

Threading his fingers through her hair, he pulled her head back, looked down into her eyes for a long, pulse-pounding moment, then lowered his mouth to hers. There was no gentle seduction here. There were only flames licking at them both. Fire erupting, engulfing, and they each rushed at the inferno, throwing themselves into the maelstrom like so much kindling.

She lifted her legs, wrapping them around his hips. He cupped her behind, holding her in place so that her body cradled his. He felt her eagerness and shared it. All he wanted was her and he knew that he had to get her back to the hotel. Fast. But first...

Gianni tore his mouth from hers, and grabbed a gulp of air like a drowning man breaching the water's surface. Looking down into her eyes, he said, "Let's get Jean Luc tucked away, then we'll—"

Her gaze shifted beyond him. "He's gone."

"What?" Still holding her, he turned to where he'd left the other man sprawled on the sand. But there was nothing. In the moments Gianni had lost himself in Marie, Jean Luc had disappeared. "Damn it. He's long gone by now."

She cupped his cheek and turned his face back to her. "Who cares?"

Surprise flickered through him for a second. Jean Luc had been the focus of her attention since she'd first come to him. Now, though, seeing the heat in her eyes, feeling the trembles wracking her body, he knew she was feeling what he was. The only thing that mattered right now was what was between them.

"You're right," he said, dropping a quick, hard kiss on her mouth. "Let's go."

He set her down, took her hand and led her back through the darkness toward the hotel. The echoes of music and laughter followed them, drifting from the showroom, but neither of them paid attention. They were focused on the hunger driving them.

In minutes, Gianni was leading her into the suite they'd shared for days. He slammed the door shut, turned to her and she jumped into his arms, as breathlessly impatient as he was. He held her close, and as she wrapped her legs around his waist, he skimmed his hands up beneath the dark green silk shirt she wore.

She sighed and arched her back as his hands cupped her breasts through the lace of her bra. He felt her nipples pebble into his palms and he nearly groaned with the satisfaction rolling through him. Damn, it felt as if he'd waited years for the touch of her skin beneath his hands.

"Gotta have you," he whispered, dragging his mouth down the slim column of her neck, nibbling as he went.

"Yes," she answered breathlessly. "Oh, yes."

Setting her on her feet, he pulled that silky top up and over her head then slid her bra straps down her arms and let the filmy fabric drop to the floor. Then she reached to unbutton his shirt and Gianni helped her with that, in a rush to feel her skin against his. When their clothes were on the floor, he tipped her back onto the mattress and when she fell, a startled laugh shot from her throat.

Gianni grinned, stretched out alongside her and immediately ran his hands up and down her body, following every luscious curve. She reached for him and pulled him down for a kiss, parting her lips for him, taking him into her heat. His tongue slicked against hers in an erotic, desperate tangle of need and desire.

Her fingernails scraped across his back and he felt each scratch like tiny flames. He swept one hand down her body to the juncture of her thighs and she opened her legs to him, inviting him to touch, explore, caress. Gianni groaned into her mouth, letting her heat spiral through his body and pump back into hers. They were linked by a slender thread of desire that wove itself around them so tightly, they couldn't have been separated even if they had wanted it.

Tearing his lips from hers, he dipped his head to take first one hardened nipple and then the other into his mouth. He licked and sucked and pulled at each one until she was writhing beneath him. He cupped her heat, rubbing the heel of his hand against that most sensitive spot. She whimpered and he groaned with his body's demand to be inside her, to feel that wet heat surrounding him, drawing him deeper, tighter.

He touched her again, pushing first one finger and then two into her depths and her hips came up off the bed, moving into his touch instinctively. He lifted his head, looked down at her and saw the wildness in her eyes. She rocked her hips into his touch, needing more and not afraid to reach for the climax that hovered so close. Gianni wanted this. Wanted to watch her shatter.

Wanted to see her eyes glaze over with the kind of passion only he could give her.

So he redoubled his stroking caresses, pushing his fingers deeper and faster, he created the sort of friction that was designed to drive them both out of their minds with want. She moved with him, gasping for air, whispering, "Yes, Gianni. Yes. Please."

"Take this from me, *cara*," he told her, voice tight and low. "Come for me and let me see you."

She opened her eyes, stared up into his and nodded. Breath straining, she moved into his hand, over and over again. Her bare feet slid on the silky duvet beneath them, but neither of them really noticed. They were wrapped up in each other and the moment hurtling toward Marie.

"Please, Gianni. I need. I need…"

"I know, *cara*. I see what you need." His thumb rolled over that hard bud of flesh at the heart of her and as he did, she shrieked, calling out his name. Her hips rocked wildly and her breath was strangled as she moved through the climax that was tearing her apart.

He watched it all and felt his own heart fill. His desire pumped harder, faster with every shattered breath she expelled. He felt her body tightening and convulsing around his fingers and before the last of those tremors had ended, Gianni made his move.

Marie was blind.

No, she thought with a shocked gasp. Not blind. Eyes closed. *Oh, my.* Her body was shaking, trembling from her head to her feet, and her skin felt like she'd been electrocuted. She felt hot all over as if she had a fever, yet the silk duvet beneath her felt cool. She was actually buzzing and the ripples of that climax were still shaking through her when she opened her eyes in time to see Gianni reach into the bedside table drawer. He pulled out a condom, ripped it open and sheathed himself in seconds.

Then he came back to her and sheathed himself in *her*.

"Gianni!"

He was so big. So hard. He filled her completely and she was so sensitive still from that mind-altering climax, she had another orgasm just from the friction of her body stretching to accommodate his.

She clutched at his shoulders, lifted her legs and wrapped them tight around his hips, holding him to her until those tremors could ease enough to make breathing less difficult. But he wouldn't be held still. He pushed deeper and her body lit up like a neon sign in the darkness.

And then he moved in her, sliding in and out of her depths with an increased rhythm that she raced frantically to meet. Over and over again, he advanced and retreated, leaving her body quivering with reawakened need. She wouldn't have believed it possible to feel *more* than she already had, but Marie looked up into Gianni's dark eyes and knew that they'd only begun.

He was lighting her up, from head to toe. His touch electrified her. His gaze was powerful, holding hers, demanding that she see him and watch as the two of them together again created something uncontrollable and wonderful. She was drowning in those eyes. She was burning up from his touch and when this climax hit her, it was so much bigger, so much more overwhelming, all Marie could do was hold on to him and ride the sensations that carried her into a world where completion was just the beginning.

Her own body was still shaking when she felt him surrender to the inevitable and fall, crashing into her arms.

"We have to talk." Marie sat up on the bed, pushed her hair out of her eyes and looked at the naked man sprawled in gorgeous splendor beside her.

He snorted a laugh. "Why is it women always have to talk after sex?"

Sex? That had been way more than just sex. At least to Marie. It had been life-altering. Amazing. Just this side of miraculous. But obviously, she wouldn't be mentioning that to Gianni. Wow, just looking at him lying there atop the sea-foam-green duvet made her want to jump him. But she fought for control and finally found some.

"Come, *cara*," he said, holding one hand out to her in a sexy invitation she really wanted to accept.

But first things first.

"Gianni, what about Jean Luc?"

"Ahh…" he sighed, grumbled something in Italian under his breath and then looked at her and shrugged. "He's gone, *cara*. Even he is not foolish enough to stay on the island when he knows that we're aware of him."

"I know that," she said, glancing at the French doors and the starlit night beyond. "What I want to know is what we're going to do now?"

"About what?"

"Our little charade, Gianni." A soft wind blew through the terrace doors and slid across her bare skin like a soft caress. "Your family knows the truth, Jean Luc is gone, what do we do now?"

He went up on one elbow, reached for her hand and stroked his thumb across her knuckles, sending new flashes of anticipation shooting through her. "What we had planned at the start of this. True, we no longer have to lie to my family, but I still have to watch this jewelry show for Interpol."

"And then?"

"Then we find Jean Luc, get your necklace back and you give me the evidence you still hold against my family. Nothing has changed, *cara*." He gave her a slow smile and tugged at her hand until she came closer, then he rolled her beneath him and bent to lavish attention on her breasts.

She sighed and held his head, watching as he suckled her and even through the pleasure he aroused in her, she could only think, *You're so wrong, Gianni. Everything has changed.*

Ten

"That was good work." Rico nodded to himself as he watched Franklin Hicks walk a handcuffed man to one of the tourist launches at the dock.

White clouds sailed across a blue sky while boaters were out on the ocean enjoying the day. Fishing boats creaked with the motion of the waves and from somewhere nearby, music drifted from a radio.

"He made it surprisingly easy," Gianni said with a snort of derision. Marie stood beside him and when he draped one arm around her shoulders, he felt her stiffen slightly before relaxing into his touch.

But then it had been this way between them since the night they first had sex. There was a closeness there, but also a wall that seemed to grow thicker and more impenetrable with the passage of time. In the last two days they had come together many times and each time had been more amazing than the one before.

He hadn't tired of her as he had so many women in his past. He'd assumed that as always, once the initial hunger had been satisfied, the need for her would ease. Instead, his desire had only increased until it was now a knot of need lodged constantly in the pit of his belly. He couldn't assuage it and couldn't ignore it.

It seemed that Marie felt the same. She was eager and passionate in their lovemaking but when it was done, she retreated into a corner of herself that he simply couldn't reach. Although, he added silently, maybe it was that he didn't really *want* to reach her. They had been through a lot together in the last week and yet, there were boundaries that neither of them could or would cross.

She was only with him because she had blackmailed him. She threatened his family and though he had the feeling she wouldn't see his father imprisoned, how could he be sure? How could he trust her? And what difference did trust make, his brain argued. They weren't a real couple. They were only together temporarily and when their time was done, they would each return to their opposite sides of the world and go back to the lives they knew best.

If that sounded empty to him, he ignored it.

"What gave this thief away?" Rico wondered aloud as they stood at the dock, watching Franklin's prisoner being loaded onto the launch boat.

"I noticed that he wasn't looking at the jewelry being displayed," Marie said. "But he *was* checking the camera angles—and when he thought no one was watching, he was taking photos with his phone."

Rico frowned. "Photographs were expressly forbidden inside the showroom."

"Thieves notoriously don't follow orders," Gianni said wryly.

Rico's frown only deepened. "That was it then, watching him check out the security?"

"That and the fact that he had a laser pen in his suit coat pocket," Gianni said.

"How do you know that?" Rico asked, eyes narrowing on him.

"When Marie told me about him, I picked his pockets."

"Oh, for—" Irritated, Rico stomped off a few feet, then came right back. "You swore you wouldn't steal anything."

"Stealing from a thief doesn't count," Gianni said.

He watched his brother-in-law fight for control and nearly smiled when the other man finally muttered, "Fine. Explain to me why you were worried about a laser pen?"

Gianni met his gaze. "It is a relatively new thing discovered by hackers. A laser pen can be used to hack a computer, picking up on keystrokes most often used and allowing the hacker to slide into your computer system with ease."

"I don't understand," Rico admitted and he didn't look happy about it.

Marie continued Gianni's explanation. "If he hacked your security cameras, he would be able to slip into the showroom at night, unnoticed. There wouldn't be a security breach because he'd have your codes."

Rico blew out a disgusted breath and shoved both hands into his pockets. "And the safes? How would he have gotten past them?"

"There was a safe amplifier in his room," Marie said,

turning her face into the wind, letting it push her hair into the tangle that Gianni loved best.

"Safe amplifier?" Rico repeated.

"It's a kind of high-tech stethoscope," Gianni explained with a little sigh of envy. He thought about the rush he used to experience when cracking a safe. Of course, all Corettis were trained the old-fashioned way and most of them could get any safe open in minutes without the help of gadgetry. Still, sometimes new toys were fun to use. "Earphones connected to an electronic device will amplify the sounds of the pins falling into place. A talented thief could get into any safe in a very short time with a tool like that."

"Key word there being *talented*," Marie said.

"Yes," Gianni agreed. "The thief we caught was less than expert in his field. As evidenced by the fact that I could pick his pockets in a crowded room and he didn't notice a thing." Shaking his head in disgust, he added, "Shame, really. There's no craftsmanship anymore."

Rico just stared at him, a befuddled look on his face, but beside him, Marie chuckled and he sent her a smile. She at least understood what he was talking about. She might look at crime from the wrong side of the fence, so to speak, but she also had an implicit acknowledgement of the talents and skills required to be a successful thief.

"Speaking of less-than-talented thieves," Marie said, slipping out from under Gianni's arm to look up at Rico. "Did you ever discover how Jean Luc was able to get away?"

Gianni missed the feel of her pressed close to him, but didn't make a move to bring her back into his side. She moved away a step or two, as if needing to be standing on her own as she faced Rico with her question.

"Yeah, Franklin looked into it. He printed a still picture of Jean Luc off one of the security feeds. When he was on hotel grounds, the cameras caught him. Anyway, Franklin showed the picture around in the village and down at the docks." Rico frowned at the cluster of fishing boats gathered at the busy dock. "Finally got lucky with one of the local fishermen. Seems Jean Luc paid the fisherman to take him to St. Thomas. The man didn't realize, of course, that Jean Luc was a thief trying to escape arrest. He believed Jean Luc's story about having to go home quickly because of an emergency."

"And I'm guessing Jean Luc was very generous…." Marie said.

"Very." Rico sighed. "He paid the fisherman the equivalent of several months' earnings."

Gianni looked at Marie and saw the frustration on her features. He couldn't blame her. He didn't like it any more than she did that the slippery Frenchman had found a way to elude them. But in a way, Gianni was also glad of it. If they'd managed to hold on to Jean Luc, then they could have retrieved the stolen necklace that much sooner, which would only cut down on the time he had left with Marie. And he wanted every moment he had with her. He wasn't ready to end this…relationship.

God. His instincts recoiled from the very word. He had never been a man who looked for commitment. The life he lived had hardly been a good fit for an everyday home life. Instead, he'd enjoyed women here and there and then left them behind when it was time to move on. And he'd never wasted a moment's thought on any of them, once they were out of his life.

Marie would be different, he knew. He would think of her. Remember her. And ache for her. Not something he was comfortable admitting, but at the same time, it wasn't something he could deny—at least not to himself.

He'd gone into this situation with Marie knowing it would be temporary, but somehow that had seemed so much simpler when this began. Now, temporary was suddenly feeling far too…temporary.

"So," Marie said glumly, "we have no idea where he went after he was on St. Thomas."

"None," Rico agreed. "Once the fisherman dropped him at the docks, Jean Luc could have gone anywhere. My guess is, straight to the airport. But from there, who knows where he headed."

Gianni was watching Marie and saw several different emotions flash across her face, one after the other. She looked up at him. "Do you think he went home? To Monaco?"

"I don't know," he admitted. "Probably, though there's no way to know for sure until we go there looking for him."

She nodded and chewed at her bottom lip.

"You're staying until the end of the jewelry exhibition, though?"

Gianni glanced at Rico briefly. "Yes. I assured Interpol I would be on site and I wouldn't want to disappoint my new employers."

Rico smiled. "I guess not. I'm glad to hear it, though. Having extra eyes on the show has already paid off." He looked at the launch that had fired up moments before and was already pulling away from the dock, carrying Franklin Hicks and the would-be thief to the authorities on St. Thomas. "I'll see you both back at the showroom this afternoon?"

"Yes," Gianni said, his gaze fixed on Marie. "We'll be there."

"Paulo and your father should be arriving tonight for the christening tomorrow," Rico said.

"Right." Gianni couldn't look away from the green-eyed gaze that stared into his with concentration.

"Okay." Rico laughed under his breath. "I'm going back to the hotel. I'll see you both there in an hour?"

"We'll see you then," Marie said.

"Fine." Rico took a step or two from them, then stopped and turned back. "You know, you two make quite a team."

"What?" Gianni asked.

"What?" Marie said at the same time.

Rico laughed again, this time louder and with real pleasure. "Like I said. Quite a team."

"What kind of team do you think?" Gianni asked, one corner of his mouth tipping up. "Sherlock and Watson?"

Her lips curved and light seemed to gleam in her eyes. "I'm thinking more Turner and Hooch."

He frowned, until he remembered the movie she was referring to. "Ah, but darling, you're so much prettier than any mastiff."

She laughed as he'd intended and when he took her hand and threaded her arm through his, she leaned into him and whispered, "You're very funny. But if we're Sherlock and Watson, you are *so* Watson."

The following day was the christening and Marie wished she were anywhere but there. Honestly, from the moment Paulo Coretti and his father had arrived on the island, Paulo had made no secret of the fact that he didn't much like Marie.

They'd all had dinner together the night before in Rico and Teresa's suite and she'd caught Paulo's suspicious-angry-curious gaze on her more than once. But he hadn't said much to her beyond a grunt of greeting. Until today.

Now, they all were once again gathered in Rico and Teresa's living room before leaving for the small island church. And Paulo's reticence from the night before was long gone.

Briefly, she flinched under his hard stare and then reminded herself that she wasn't the bad guy here. Well, she reconsidered, to him, she probably was. She had evidence against his father and had blackmailed his brother. Her gaze shifted to where Gianni sat, calm and seemingly indifferent while his younger brother ranted.

Looking at Paulo objectively, Marie could see the resemblance between the brothers, but to her, Gianni was gorgeous. He was taller, leaner somehow despite the muscles she'd spent the last two nights defining with her fingertips—and his temperament wasn't nearly as volatile as Paulo's.

Marie shifted uncomfortably on the couch and felt as if she were on display. All eyes seemed turned to her and while she couldn't blame them, she wasn't enjoying the attention.

Teresa sat on the couch beside her father, Nick, who held his first grandchild in his arms. Rico was standing at the bar, looking as though he wanted to stuff a sock in Paulo's mouth to keep him quiet. And Gianni lounged on the couch beside Marie, his features carefully blank.

For two days, Marie and Gianni had been together in every way possible. There was no more pretense between them, just passion. Marie had given up trying to sort out what was happening to her. All she could do was admit to what she felt when she was with Gianni and enjoy it as long as she could.

But it wasn't just the passion she was enjoying. It was simply being with him. Marie had loved it all. Working with him, sleeping with him, having him reach for her in the middle of the night to make love slowly in the shadowy light. She knew nothing was solved between them, she knew there was still Jean Luc to deal with, the return of the Contessa and the evidence against his father. But for two days, she'd managed to not worry about the future and just enjoy the now, as Gianni had once said.

But this *now* was far less enjoyable.

"She holds evidence against our father," Paulo was saying in a voice loud enough to grab her attention, "and yet, she sits here with us as though she belongs." He threw both hands up in the air, then stalked across the living room to the wet bar, where Rico had a cold beer waiting for him.

Those words slapped at her, whether Gianni's brother knew it or not. She didn't belong and she knew it. She hadn't belonged anywhere since her father died. And while the Corettis were circling the wagons to protect their own from her, all she could really feel was envy at what they had. Even though they didn't live near each other, though they might only see each other a few times a year, the closeness between them was easy for an outsider to acknowledge.

And that's what she was, she reminded herself. Despite what she and Gianni had been to each other for the last few days, she was an outsider and always would be.

"Paulo," Teresa said, trying to calm the waters, "Marie's not going to turn Papa in."

Marie looked at the other woman gratefully. She'd at

least made a friend here this week, she told herself, and she'd miss Teresa when all this ended.

Paulo laughed, a harsh, short shot of sound. "And for this you take her word? The word of a cop?"

"I'm not a cop anymore," Marie said, finally entering the Coretti fray to defend herself. She sent Gianni, still seated casually on the sofa, an angry glare for keeping quiet. It wasn't as though she needed rescuing, but it would have been nice to hear him say something in her favor. Apparently, though, she was doomed to disappointment there.

Turning back to face his brother she continued. "I'm not even employed, thanks to Jean Luc Baptiste."

Paulo took a long pull of his beer. "Please. You are a cop inside—" he slapped his chest with one hand for emphasis "—where it matters most. You traveled the world to find evidence against us, then to wind Gianni up in your scheme to find Jean Luc and get back a necklace stolen from under your nose. That sense of justice is all cop."

She stood up, facing him on her feet. "You say that like it's an insult, but it's not. My father was a cop and his father before him. You're proud of your family, yes?"

His eyes narrowed, but he nodded.

"So am I," she snapped. "I get that you're angry about my being here, but maybe attacking me isn't the best way to handle it."

Paulo fumed silently, but she caught the gleam of respect in his eyes as he looked at her. And that, she told herself, was probably as good as she was going to get from him.

Stunned silence stretched out for a few seconds before Gianni began applauding, slowly and loudly. One by one, everyone turned to look at him. He stood up, pulled Marie to his side and held her there when she might have squirmed out of his reach. "That's enough, Paulo. Marie is with me and you won't say another word to her about any of this."

The other man took a breath as if about to argue, but Gianni cut him off. "I mean it. What's between Marie and I will remain between the two of us."

"And the evidence she holds?"

Marie shifted uncomfortably. Gianni's arm around her tightened.

"It is for me to worry about."

"Easy enough to say when it is Papa who will go to prison."

Marie grimaced and shifted her gaze to where the older man sat on the couch softly jiggling his sleeping grandson in his arms. As if he knew everyone was looking at him, Nick spoke, never taking his gaze off the baby.

"Prison is not so much a thing to fear, Paulo. And if this lovely young woman believes it is the right thing to do, then she will turn the photo over to the *polizia* in Italy and it will be done."

"Papa—" Paulo stopped when his father fired one quick glare at him.

"Enough. As Gianni says, all will be as it will be. For today, this is the christening of my grandson and I will allow nothing to spoil it." His voice was firm and low as he asked of the room in general, "Is that understood?"

Muttered agreements rolled through the room and when Gianni gave Marie a hard squeeze, she leaned into him, grateful for the support. She looked up at him and he smiled. That's when she figured out that he'd waited for her to speak up for herself. To stand against Paulo and set a tone with his younger brother.

It was just one more thing she loved about him. Gianni would be her white knight if she needed one, but he also had enough confidence in her to stand back and enjoy watching her take care of herself.

She took a breath and let her mind wander as the Coretti family stood and readied to leave for the church. Working with Gianni at the jewelry show had been fun. As had catching that thief—being the "team," as Rico had called them. She loved that Gianni could make her laugh. Loved that he respected her opinions. Loved that he looked at her through eyes glowing with desire. Loved that—oh, God.

She loved him.

How had it happened so quickly? Heck, how had it happened at all? Gianni Coretti represented everything she'd fought against her entire adult life. He was a thief— reformed or not—and he was proud of it. He came from a family that flaunted laws in every country they visited. He was everything she should have avoided—and everything she wanted.

She was in very deep trouble.

The small Catholic church stood at the end of the village. Locals had built the chapel from river stone brought in from all over the island and the result was a place that felt both warm and sacred. The baptismal font was a huge bowl hand-carved from one of the ancient banyan trees and sanded until it looked like honey-colored satin. Stained glass windows over the altar sent shards of ruby, golden and sapphire sunlight drifting over the people gathered at the font as the island priest blessed Matteo King.

Marie still had that outsider feeling, but Gianni seemed to sense it in her. He made a point of holding her hand or draping his arm over her shoulder, drawing her into the center of things even when her mind and heart told her to pull away.

The Corettis stood together as a family, huddled around the tiny child, who was the star of the show. Rico's cousin, Sean King, and his wife, Melinda, were godparents and Nick Coretti kept their two children amused during the ceremony. It was all very simple, straightforward and lovely in a way that touched Marie's heart and lodged a knot of sentiment in her throat.

As she watched the family's closeness, their commitment to each other, Marie finally realized that she couldn't go through with the plan that had brought her here. Her gaze moved over Nick, an older, charming man who smiled and whispered with two tiny restless children. He was a thief, yes, but he was so much more than that, too.

Those shades of gray infiltrating her world were becoming difficult to ignore. The stark universe of right and wrong she'd always inhabited seemed so narrow now, she couldn't imagine how she'd lived like that for so long. She couldn't send Nick to prison. She'd never be able to live with herself thinking of him locked away in some sterile, awful cell, unable to see the family he so clearly adored.

Gianni's hand squeezed hers and she knew she was through blackmailing him. Taking a deep breath, she promised herself that once they were back at the hotel, she'd give Gianni the evidence she had against his father and tell him he had nothing to worry about from her. She couldn't blackmail a man she loved—especially not by threatening the family that meant so much to him. Her mind was so busy, she hardly noticed the rest of the ceremony.

By the time the baptism was over and the small party wandered out into the sunlight, laughing and talking, Marie felt as though she'd run an emotional marathon. She needed air. Space. Time to separate her heart from her mind and try to figure out what to do next with her life.

But she didn't get that time. Instead, Gianni bent his head to hers and whispered, "Teresa has lunch planned for all of us. But after that, I think we should go to our room for a...*nap*."

Marie looked up at him and found the smile she knew he needed. Then giving in to the urge to touch him, she reached up and stroked her fingertips across his cheek. None of this was going to end well. She knew it. There was just no possible way out of this situation without ending up as the walking wounded.

Yet, she couldn't deny herself another chance to have Gianni's body deep inside hers. So for the *now,* she told herself firmly, she would do what she wanted, needed to do. One more night with him. She knew what she had to do.

All she needed was the courage to do it.

Their bodies still locked together in the aftermath of the storm, Marie trembled with the force of the orgasm still rippling through her bloodstream, fogging her mind.

She threaded her fingers through his thick black hair and let the softness glide against her skin, making another sensory memory that she would carry with her always. Breathing harsh and heavy, he looked down into her eyes for a long moment as their heartbeats slowly returned to normal. Finally, though, he rolled to one side of her, propped himself up on an elbow and asked, "Do you want to tell me what you're thinking?"

"Not really," she admitted, trepidation and misery already rising up inside her.

"Marie…"

She bit her lip and when he reached out one hand to her, she slipped away, sliding off the edge of the huge bed, dragging the sheet with her. Holding it up in front of her like a flimsy shield, she forced herself to say what she didn't want to. "I'm leaving, Gianni."

Frowning slightly in confusion, he shook his head and said, "Yes. We will both be leaving once the exhibition is over."

"No." She shook her head and lifted her chin. "I meant, I'm leaving now."

"Now?" He sat up to stare at her. "Why would you do that?"

"Because it's the only thing I can do," she said, not expecting him to understand. Wow, could she have handled the beginning of this conversation more awkwardly? "I'm trying to say it's over, Gianni. Jean Luc is gone and now that he knows we're together, his guard will be up and we'll never get the Contessa back."

He pushed off the bed, marched around it, proudly naked and not bothering to cover himself. Although, she thought wildly, why would he? If there ever was a man built to walk around nude, it was Gianni Coretti. Just looking at him made her mouth water and her hands itch to touch all that bronzed skin.

But the expression on his face was forbidding. "I have told you I will retrieve the necklace and I will."

"I know you would try," she said, trying to soothe him, but apparently failing when his expression only darkened.

"Try?" he repeated. "I am Gianni Coretti. If I tell you I will do something, I do it."

A harsh, strained chuckle escaped her throat. He was so impossibly arrogant and self-confident. So sure that he could do anything—why did that only make her love him more? "I'm telling you I don't want you to. I think it's best for both of us if we just go back to our lives and… forget we ever met."

Gianni was speechless. For the first time in his life he had absolutely no idea what to say. His quick wit had failed him when he needed it most. He had nothing to fight against the sad and miserable expression on her face. Her eyes told him everything. She had already said goodbye, with her body. He realized that now. Even while he had been making love to her, she was letting him go, mentally returning to her own life, far from his. Now it was only left for her mind to do the same.

But he wasn't ready. He didn't want to forget her. Didn't want to see her leave. Not yet. Even as those thoughts and more raced through his brain, he admitted silently that he hadn't counted on this. Hadn't thought that a woman he'd caught burgling his home could come to mean so much to him in so little time. Hadn't thought to guard the heart he had been sure was unreachable.

And now, he would have to pay for that miscalculation.

Thinking fast, he approached her, one long stride at a time. "Come with me to London," he blurted out. "We will stay at my home until we have the right plan for getting the necklace."

She shook her head sadly and that just annoyed him. How dare she give up and walk away? He took another step closer and noted that she took a step back in response. He ignored it.

"Then we will go to Monaco together," he said, hoping to entice her. "As Rico pointed out we make a good team. Together, we will relieve Jean Luc of the jewels he stole. Together, *cara*."

A small, sad smile curved her lips briefly. "London. Monaco. You. It all sounds wonderful."

"Then stay," he demanded.

"No. I can't."

"Tell me why." He reached her, dropped both hands on her shoulders and held on to her when she would have tried to get away from him again. "Tell me."

She tipped her head back to meet his eyes and he read regret in those beautiful grass-green depths.

"Because if you tried to steal back the necklace I asked you to get and then you were caught and sent to prison I'd never be able to live with myself."

He laughed, a short, sharp bark of laughter shot through with derision. "Caught? Corettis are not caught. Ever."

"There's always a first time and I won't risk it," she said quickly.

"There is more to this, that you aren't saying," he muttered, searching her eyes, knowing that her feelings and emotions were crashing around inside her head and heart as much as his own were inside himself.

"Yes," she admitted, still looking up at him even as she pulled herself free of his grasp. "Gianni, you're a thief. Yes, yes," she said quickly before he could correct her, "*former* thief. But still a thief in your heart. Just as I'm always going to be a cop in mine."

"What does any of that signify?" He narrowed his gaze on her.

She pushed her hair back from her face, blew out a breath and said, "In the last week, so many things have changed for me. The world I used to know so well now seems foreign to me after meeting you. Your family. This place." She shook her head and sighed. "But this isn't real. It's not my world. Any of it. I was raised with respect for the law. It's who I am. It's practically in my DNA. If I lose that, then who am I?"

"Why would you lose what you are?" His words were tight as he reached for her again and came up empty when she sidestepped him.

She glanced down at the ring on her finger and slowly slid it off and held it in the palm of her hand. "This ring pretty much says it all. It belongs to some woman I've never met. It was stolen from her and held as a trophy then given to me to pretend a life that didn't exist." Sadly, she looked up at him as she took his hand and placed the ring in it. "It was all make-believe, Gianni. It was just more of the *now* that you're so fond of."

He felt the heavy weight of the diamond in his hand and thought he might crush it to dust if he gave in to the urge he felt to smash his fist over it. "There's nothing wrong with *now, cara,*" he said.

"No." She walked past him and he didn't try to stop her. What would have been the point? "But sooner or later, *now* becomes the past and all you're left with is the memory."

Gianni gritted his teeth and looked down at the ring

she'd returned to him. For the first time since the night he'd stolen it, the diamond held no beauty. It might as well have been a piece of glass. Cold. Lifeless.

"And Gianni?"

He looked up at her, paused just inside the adjoining bathroom.

"I'll leave the photos of your father with you. I don't want you to worry. Nick won't go to prison because of me. Not now. Not ever."

When she closed herself up in the bathroom, Gianni was left alone in the twilight of the shadowed bedroom. It shamed him to admit that while she had been saying goodbye…he hadn't given his father's freedom a single thought.

Eleven

"I can't believe you're leaving." Teresa hugged Marie tightly the next morning.

"I have to go while I can still force myself to do it," Marie told her. Her conversation with Gianni the night before still rang in her mind. As did the memory of him silently getting dressed and leaving the suite. He hadn't come back all night. So Marie had been alone in the darkened suite for hours, with nothing to do but rethink every moment she'd spent with Gianni.

How had she done so much, *felt* so much, in little more than a week? It should have been impossible to love like that so quickly. And yet…walking away from Gianni was the hardest thing she'd ever had to do. Saying goodbye to Teresa wasn't much easier.

The penthouse apartment was flooded with sunlight, glancing off the jewel-toned colors that filled the room.

Funny, but Teresa and Rico's home was so familiar to her now that Marie knew she'd miss it, too, when she was gone. As she would miss her friend.

"But you love Gianni," Teresa said softly, watching Marie's face for a reaction.

"I do." She shook her head. "At least, I think I do, but it's barely been more than a week since I met him. Love doesn't happen that quickly."

Teresa laughed a little. "How long does it take, I wonder? One week? A year? Ten? Or perhaps only a moment when eyes meet. No, Marie. There's no hard-and-fast rule to love. It simply is. And when you find it, you know it."

True. All true. She already knew she loved Gianni, Marie had simply been trying to convince herself that she didn't. Because walking away from him was already the hardest thing she'd ever done. Admitting that she was throwing love away would only make it more difficult.

"It doesn't matter," she whispered.

"It's all that matters," Teresa argued. "And Gianni loves you, too."

Marie's head snapped up and her gaze met Teresa's. Hope billowed inside like a parachute catching the wind, but just as quickly, that hopeful wind died and the parachute crashed back to earth. "You don't know that," she said.

"Of course I know. My brother is easy enough to read when you've spent a lifetime doing it," Teresa told her. "I see him with you. I hear more laughter from him than I've heard in years. Seen more…excitement with the world around him. And that is because of you."

If Marie believed that, maybe she could find a way to make this work. Sadly though, she didn't believe it. He'd asked her to stay. To go to London and Monaco with him.

But that invitation without love behind it felt…hollow. Gianni hadn't said anything about love—of course, her mind taunted, neither had she. But the point, she argued silently, was that love had never been put on the table, so to speak. They had had an affair. A fling. A summer caper of chasing jewel thieves, where they'd lived lives of sensual abandon, putting the outside world on hold while they indulged themselves in a fantasy.

Now the fantasy was over.

"He doesn't love me," she said firmly, wanting to convince herself of that to make the leaving a bit easier. "And that's okay, Teresa. Really. I'll be fine, I just… have to go."

"My brother is an *idiota*," Teresa said softly, using an Italian word that Marie had no trouble translating.

Wryly, she smiled and hugged the other woman again. "When Matteo wakes from his nap, kiss him for me, will you?"

"Of course," Teresa promised. "And you will come back? To visit me?"

"I will," Marie lied and hoped that this time her lying skills had been believable. Marie could never come back to Tesoro. The memories of her time here with Gianni would make it impossible to so much as breathe. "And if you ever get to New York, call me, okay?"

"I will." Teresa sighed a little as if she, too, realized that the chances of their seeing each other again were slim to none.

Then Marie left the penthouse while she could still make her legs work. Every step felt as if she were pulling her feet out of mud as she laboriously moved into the elevator and punched the button for the lobby. Once downstairs, her leaden legs moved her out of the hotel to the shuttle that would get her to the docks, where a launch boat was waiting to take her to St. Thomas for her flight back to grim reality.

"You should be happy!" Paulo was clearly stunned at Gianni's lack of enthusiasm over the fact that he had been able to burn the pictures of his father exiting the Van Court estate.

There was no more threat against the elder Coretti. The family was safe. The woman who had put all of this in motion was even now on her way back to the States. And yet…Gianni could find no relief inside him.

Instead, there was a tangled knot of desolation in the pit of his belly. No amount of the very good scotch Rico was providing could chase away the cold that had seeped into every vein and cell in his body. And his brain gave him no peace, either. It simply replayed that last scene with Marie over and over again, as if living through it once hadn't been enough.

He still couldn't believe she'd walked away. From *him*. No woman had ever walked out on him and he didn't like it. He'd thought for sure he could get her to stay, but he'd failed at the most important task he'd ever set himself.

"Leave him alone, Paulo," Teresa muttered.

That man laughed shortly and lifted his bottle of beer. "Why are you all acting as though you were at a funeral? She's gone. The threat is gone. It's over and done, we should be celebrating."

"Paulo," their father said softly, without taking his gaze from his oldest son, "there is much you don't know."

"For instance?"

Nick Coretti sighed, glanced at his youngest son and

said, "For instance, you have no idea what it feels like to truly love."

Gianni's head snapped up at that statement and his gaze fixed on his father. "Love? Who said anything about love?"

Nick frowned and clucked his tongue. "Apparently, no one. But you should have."

"Thank you, Papa!" Teresa gave her oldest brother a withering glare. "It's exactly what I told him an hour ago."

"And I told you to mind your own business," Gianni said softly.

Rico laughed from the end of the couch. "You think she'll do that? Do you even know your sister?" When Teresa's elbow plowed into his stomach, Rico winced, but grabbed her and pulled her up against his side.

"My family *is* my business," Teresa retorted, then stabbed her index finger at Gianni. "You should not have let her go."

His mouth twisted and his teeth clenched to keep inside all of the hot words that wanted to pour out. Looking at his baby sister, Gianni shied away from the fierce light of battle gleaming in her dark eyes. Teresa was a Coretti through and through, no matter that her last name now was King. And if she thought she was right, she wouldn't be stopped.

"What was I supposed to do?" Gianni countered, swallowing the last of his scotch, then leaning forward to set his empty glass on the coffee table in front of him. "She wanted to leave." Just saying it aloud sent ripples of shock through him.

"Of course she didn't want to go," Teresa said, exasperation coloring her words. "You are such a man, Gianni. Couldn't you look into her eyes and see she loved you?"

His heart jolted, but he wouldn't believe it. "If she loved me she would have stayed."

"Did you tell her your feelings?" Nick spoke quietly, but as always, when their father had something to say, everyone listened.

"I don't know my feelings, Papa," Gianni admitted, though it was humbling. He jumped to his feet, stalked to the terrace doors and stared out at the moonlight shattering on the water's surface. "I asked her to stay and she said no."

"You gave her no reason to stay, Gianni," his father said.

He'd offered her his home. Travel. Adventure. What more could he have said? Marie was gone. On a plane, probably close to landing in New York by now. She was alone and he wondered if she thought of him. If she regretted leaving. Anger sizzled inside him, burning at the knots in his belly until they were hot coals, blistering his soul.

"I feel such *delusione,*" Nick said on a sigh.

Gianni looked back at his father. "Disappointment, Papa? Why? I got the photos Marie had. You're safe. The family is safe."

"*Basta.* Enough." Nick waved his hand in the air, brushing away Gianni's words like so many gnats irritating him. "That woman would not have turned me in and surely you know that."

"She was a cop," Paulo said loudly enough that Nick turned to glance at him. "She would have done it, Papa."

"No." Nick shook his head solemnly. "She would not hurt Gianni so."

"Finally," Teresa muttered, "a Coretti with a brain."

Gianni shot her a fulminating stare, then shifted his gaze to his father. "This isn't about love, Papa. It's about choices and she made hers. She chose to return to New York. She couldn't separate me from the life I once lived, so she left."

"Sciocco," Nick said, pushing himself to his feet and crossing the room to face down his oldest son. "You're being foolish. You look no further than where you must to avoid seeing the truth."

Gianni laughed shortly. "I see all the truth, Papa. She chose the rigid life of black and white and right and wrong. She couldn't bend enough to see that all things are not so easily defined."

Marie was stubborn and defiant and he missed her already. Her absence tore at him, whittling away small pieces of his heart with every breath he took. Gianni knew that if nothing changed, soon he would be left with only an empty hole in his chest where his heart had once been.

He would never have believed that he could feel so much for a woman who was so far from everything he had ever known. But there it was. Without Marie here, he felt as though even the air around him was flavorless. Drawing air into his lungs was simply a necessary exercise—not the delicious torture of inhaling her scent and holding it within him. God, he couldn't even breathe without missing her.

"What have I come to?" He whispered the words low enough that only his father, standing beside him, overheard.

Nick lay one hand on his son's shoulder and squeezed. "You've come to the place I prayed you would. You've found a woman, as I once did. Your mother meant more to me than my own life. Without her I was nothing. With her, there was *everything*."

Gianni shook his head and looked at his father. "But Mama wanted you. She chose to be with you."

"Not at first." Nick winked. "She took some convincing," he mused with a tender smile on his face. "And as I remember it, persuading her was very sweet indeed."

"Persuasion." Gianni thought about that and looked back over the ocean. But instead of the endless sweep of sea and sky, he saw wide green eyes, a tumble of dark red hair and a luscious mouth curved in a secretive, lover's smile.

His eyes narrowed, his jaw clenched, he told himself that he had never once lost anything that was truly important to him. And he wasn't going to start now.

Marie slapped the side of her window air conditioner and mumbled a curse when the darn thing hiccupped, then stopped altogether. "Perfect," she muttered darkly. "Just perfect."

She crossed the narrow living room and turned her floor fan up to high. It didn't make it cooler in the stifling heat, but at least it moved the hot air around. Not much consolation, but she'd take it. Through the open windows, came the sounds of the city, a low growl of traffic, honking horns and people shouting. Summer in New York was a far cry from the lovely trade winds on Tesoro.

Back at the kitchen table, she sat down and took a sip of her iced tea and imagined it was that lovely peach drink she and Teresa had shared beside the pool. But she'd been back in New York for two weeks and it was high time she stopped thinking about her days on Tesoro.

Bad enough that every night she dreamed about Gianni and the amazing sensations she'd discovered in his arms. She woke up every morning more tired than when she went to bed and with her body burning for a release it would never know again.

She really couldn't afford to start daydreaming about her temporary trip into the world of fantasy. It was over. Done. She was back to the life she knew. The world she'd been raised to expect. And her time with Gianni was as dead as her air conditioner.

So she focused on the want ads in front of her. She needed a job, but she didn't want anything...ordinary. She wanted something that would offer her adventure, excitement—everything she'd given up to return home.

"God, I'm hopeless." She glanced down at the classified section of the paper and sighed. Not many job listings promised to expand your horizons and that's what she wanted. Marie only wished she had been able to have all of that and Gianni, too.

But she knew she'd done the right thing—the only thing—in leaving. Neither of them had mentioned love. And she couldn't have stayed with him, loving him, knowing he didn't love her back. That was just asking for misery.

But her heart ached and the thought of never seeing him again was enough to bring her to tears if she hadn't already cried herself out two weeks ago.

When the doorbell rang, she jumped up, eager for the distraction from her thoughts no matter who it might be. In a few short steps, she crossed the living room, threw open the door and then just stood there, mouth open, staring up at the man who starred nightly in her dreams.

"Gianni." His name was a whispered hush as if a part

of her were afraid of saying it too loudly in case her voice might shatter the illusion in front of her.

He looked amazing in a charcoal-gray suit with a deep blue tie. His hair was stylishly cut and the scent of him reached for her until she had to grab hold of the door frame to keep from leaping at him. He looked amazing and she knew she looked wrung out by the heat. She wore a white tank top, red shorts and she was barefoot. Oh, yes. This was fair.

"Thank you," he finally quipped when she didn't speak again. "I will come in."

He walked past her into the tiny space and Marie turned to see her apartment through his eyes. Of course, she could fit her whole place into one of the guest bedrooms in his London flat. But it was cozy and it was hers. A love seat and chair, both covered in floral fabric, were the only seating options—and both were more comfortable than anything in his place—and there was a narrow table in front of them. A few feet away was the kitchen table—also narrow—with two chairs. The kitchen was tiny, the bathroom even smaller and her bedroom was only big enough for a twin-sized bed.

But she'd made it homey and comfortable and if it wasn't so blasted hot in there at the moment, she'd be very proud of her home. "What're you doing here?"

He looked at her over his shoulder as he examined the kitchen area. "We have unfinished business."

"We do?"

Glancing down at the classified pages, he shook his head, then looked to her again. "You don't need a new job, Marie. You could have your old one back now if you wanted."

Confused, she just watched as he walked toward her

and pulled a velvet bag from the inside pocket of his suit jacket. She held her breath as he untied the neck of the bag, then bent down and spilled the contents onto her coffee table.

The Contessa glittered at her in the sunlight, each diamond winking brightly, catching the sun and shooting rainbows all around the room as if in celebration.

"Oh, my God. You did it." Marie looked from the necklace to him. "What did you do?"

He shrugged. "I went to Monaco and retrieved the necklace from Jean Luc." Gianni snorted. "He didn't even have a safe. It was simply stuffed into a drawer in his bedroom. Pitiful, really. Anyway, I wanted you to have the necklace—to salvage the reputation that is so important to you."

Her reputation was important to her. For years, it had been all she had. But Gianni meant even more to her. While she was grateful for what he'd done, a part of her also wanted to shriek. "You shouldn't have, Gianni. You might have been caught. Gone to prison."

"I'm only caught when I want to be," he told her, his gaze boring into hers.

"What's that supposed to mean?"

"I'll tell you after you answer a question." He studied her even as he reached up to loosen his tie and then his shirt collar. Frowning, he said, "It is like a fire in here."

"Air conditioner broke again."

Shrugging out of his jacket, he tossed it onto the chair beside him. "No matter. The question is, do you want your old job at the Wainwright, Marie? The Contessa's return would ensure that for you."

She wasn't as sure as he was about that. Even returning the necklace might not win her back a job that had by now been given to someone else. But that wasn't necessarily a bad thing, either. "No, I don't want that job anymore. Being able to return Abigail's necklace feels wonderful and thank you for that, even though I didn't ask you to and you shouldn't have done it."

One eyebrow quirked. "So very gracious. How I've missed it."

Marie frowned. "Anyway, traveling through Europe sort of changed things for me. I want…adventure in my life, I guess. So no, I won't be going back to my old job."

"Good to know," he said, scowling furiously as he unbuttoned his cuffs and rolled back the sleeves of his shirt. "It is *rovente* in here—scorching hot. Can you not open a window?"

"The windows *are* open."

"Santa Madre," he muttered, clearly astonished.

"Welcome to summer in the city." Marie crossed her arms over her chest and looked at him. "So, I answered your question. Now you answer mine. What did you mean you're only caught when you want to be?"

"I mean," he said, reaching out to grab her upper arms and pull her in close, *"you* are the one who caught me. And I wanted you to."

"You did?" Marie's heart overflowed in an instant and tears spilled from the corners of her eyes.

His thumbs gently brushed her tears away and a soft smile turned the corners of his mouth up. "No crying, *cara*. It cuts at me to see a strong woman cry."

She chewed at her bottom lip, took a breath and fought for control. When she thought she had it she asked, "What are you trying to say, Gianni?"

"I'm trying to tell you adventure is out there to be had. To be *shared*. By us. Together. I have missed you, *cara*."

He dropped a hard, fast kiss on her mouth. "I want you to marry me. Let Teresa throw us a wedding on Tesoro. Move to London with me—help me do something with that awful furniture."

Marie laughed unsteadily. She couldn't believe this was happening. Was this another dream?

"And, if you must be a police officer," Gianni was saying, "I have friends now in Interpol. We could work together…."

Marie was shaking, trembling from head to toe. She was happy and confused all at once. She'd convinced herself that never seeing Gianni again was the right thing to do and now she couldn't remember *why*. He was standing here in front of her, offering her the world and the chance to see it by his side. But he still hadn't given her the words she most needed to hear.

"Still no answer," he said to himself, then added, "I don't believe I've ever seen you speechless. I don't think I like it. So, perhaps this will convince you to speak to me…I love you, Marie O'Hara, daughter and grand-daughter of policemen."

"Oh, my." She laughed and lifted one hand to her mouth to try to stifle the sound.

"I love you so much," he continued with a sigh, "that I *returned* your temporary engagement ring to the woman I stole it from."

"You did?" A wide, delighted smile creased her face. He'd given up the trophy he had held on to for years. And he'd done it for her. "Oh, Gianni."

"Don't look at me as if I'm a hero," he said, shaking his head. "I didn't deliver it personally. I sent it express post and made her sign for it so that I know it was delivered."

"I can't believe you did that," she whispered, still smiling.

"Believe me, neither could Paulo." He winked. "But it was important to you and so it became important to me."

"Gianni—"

"I am not finished yet, woman," he said, a half smile touching his mouth briefly. "First you are speechless, then you interrupt. Soon it will be your turn. I've brought you this." He reached into his pocket again and this time took out a small deep red box.

Marie's fluttering heart jolted to a stop. She wouldn't have been surprised to simply keel over. But somehow she managed to keep her feet under her.

"This is what you've brought me to," he told her wryly. "I *bought* this ring especially for you. And *paid* for it. It was a rare experience."

She laughed again. God, how she'd missed laughter the last couple of weeks. Being with Gianni had made her feel more alive every moment and now that he was here again, it was as if she'd woken up from a prolonged coma or something.

"When I saw this ring in the jeweler's window in Mayfair, I knew it was meant to be yours." He opened the box. "The emerald is the exact shade of your eyes. And, it is the same size as the diamond that was so sadly returned…."

Marie's breath caught. She looked from that beautiful ring to Gianni's gorgeous eyes, shining at her with more love and emotion than she'd ever seen before and she knew that she'd been given a gift. For whatever reason, the universe at large had given her a second chance at the love of a lifetime and she wouldn't let it go this time.

Sliding that ring onto her finger, Gianni said, "Marry

me, Marie. Be my lover. My friend. Come home with me and build a family. Without you, I am nothing."

"Gianni, I've missed you so much." She went up onto her toes to kiss him and when she was finished, she said, "I love you, too. I think I have right from that first night in your apartment."

He grinned. "On our first anniversary, you must lie on the floor in that short skirt again...." He sighed dramatically and slapped one hand to his heart. "I was lost from the moment I saw your beautiful legs sticking out from under my bed."

Marie laughed and leaped at him, wrapping her arms around his neck and holding on as if she'd never let him go. Gianni's arms came around her middle and he spun her in a tight circle. When he pulled back to look into her eyes, he said, "I would like nothing more than to take you to bed, my love. But not in this sauna. Shall we go to my hotel?"

"Where are you staying?"

"The Waldorf," he said with a casual ease that had Marie's eyes narrowing suspiciously.

She kept her gaze on him. "I happen to know the Waldorf Astoria has an excellent security system...."

He only smiled. "As I keep telling you, *cara*, I am a *former* thief."

Shaking her head, Marie looked up at the man she loved and grinned. "The cop and the thief. Two sides of one coin."

"It's practically poetic," he agreed, then kissed her once more. "Besides, I may be the thief, but you, *cara*, stole my heart."

* * * * *

If you loved THE FIANCÉE CAPER,
pick up Melinda and Sean's story

THE TEMPORARY MRS. KING

and Rico and Teresa's story

HER RETURN TO KING'S BED

Available now from
USA TODAY bestselling author
Maureen Child and Harlequin Desire!

COMING NEXT MONTH FROM

HARLEQUIN
Desire

Available September 2, 2014

#2323 A TEXAN IN HER BED
Lone Star Legends • by Sara Orwig
When Texas billionaire Wyatt Milan learns that stunning TV personality Destiny Jones intends to stir up a century-long family feud, his plan to stop her leads to a seduction that threatens his guarded heart.

#2324 REUNITED WITH THE LASSITER BRIDE
Dynasties: The Lassiters • by Barbara Dunlop
Angelica Lassiter thought she'd lost Evan forever after her grandfather's will wrecked their engagement. But when their best friends' wedding forces them to walk down the aisle—as best man and maid of honor—sparks fly!

#2325 SINGLE MAN MEETS SINGLE MOM
Billionaires and Babies • by Jules Bennett
When Hollywood agent Ian is stranded with single mom Cassie, their desire spirals out of control. But to be the man and father Cassie and her daughter need, Ian will have to face his dark past.

#2326 HEIR TO SCANDAL
Secrets of Eden • by Andrea Laurence
When congressman Xander Langston returns home, he wants a second chance with his high school sweetheart, Rose. But will the secrets they're keeping—including the truth about Rose's ten-year-old son—ruin everything?

#2327 MATCHED TO HER RIVAL
Happily Ever After, Inc. • by Kat Cantrell
To prove to cynical media mogul Dax that she's no fraud, matchmaker Elise challenges him to become a client. Except her supposedly infallible match software spits out *her* name as his perfect match!

#2328 NOT THE BOSS'S BABY
The Beaumont Heirs • by Sarah M. Anderson
Chadwick Beaumont is tired of doing what everyone wants him to do. It's time he did what he wants. And he wants his secretary, Serena Chase—pregnant or not!

YOU CAN FIND MORE INFORMATION ON UPCOMING HARLEQUIN® TITLES, FREE EXCERPTS AND MORE AT WWW.HARLEQUIN.COM.

HDCNM0814

REQUEST YOUR FREE BOOKS!
2 FREE NOVELS PLUS 2 FREE GIFTS!

HARLEQUIN®

Desire

ALWAYS POWERFUL, PASSIONATE AND PROVOCATIVE

YES! Please send me 2 FREE Harlequin Desire® novels and my 2 FREE gifts (gifts are worth about $10). After receiving them, if I don't wish to receive any more books, I can return the shipping statement marked "cancel." If I don't cancel, I will receive 6 brand-new novels every month and be billed just $4.55 per book in the U.S. or $4.99 per book in Canada. That's a savings of at least 13% off the cover price! It's quite a bargain! Shipping and handling is just 50¢ per book in the U.S. and 75¢ per book in Canada.* I understand that accepting the 2 free books and gifts places me under no obligation to buy anything. I can always return a shipment and cancel at any time. Even if I never buy another book, the two free books and gifts are mine to keep forever.

225/326 HDN F4ZC

Name _____ (PLEASE PRINT) _____

Address _____ Apt. # _____

City _____ State/Prov. _____ Zip/Postal Code _____

Signature (if under 18, a parent or guardian must sign) _____

Mail to the **Harlequin® Reader Service:**
IN U.S.A.: P.O. Box 1867, Buffalo, NY 14240-1867
IN CANADA: P.O. Box 609, Fort Erie, Ontario L2A 5X3

Want to try two free books from another line?
Call 1-800-873-8635 or visit www.ReaderService.com.

* Terms and prices subject to change without notice. Prices do not include applicable taxes. Sales tax applicable in N.Y. Canadian residents will be charged applicable taxes. Offer not valid in Quebec. This offer is limited to one order per household. Not valid for current subscribers to Harlequin Desire books. All orders subject to credit approval. Credit or debit balances in a customer's account(s) may be offset by any other outstanding balance owed by or to the customer. Please allow 4 to 6 weeks for delivery. Offer available while quantities last.

Your Privacy—The Harlequin® Reader Service is committed to protecting your privacy. Our Privacy Policy is available online at www.ReaderService.com or upon request from the Harlequin Reader Service.

We make a portion of our mailing list available to reputable third parties that offer products we believe may interest you. If you prefer that we not exchange your name with third parties, or if you wish to clarify or modify your communication preferences, please visit us at www.ReaderService.com/consumerschoice or write to us at Harlequin Reader Service Preference Service, P.O. Box 9062, Buffalo, NY 14269. Include your complete name and address.

HD13R

SPECIAL EXCERPT FROM

 HARLEQUIN
™

Desire

Read on for a sneak peek at
Barbara Dunlop's
REUNITED WITH THE LASSITER BRIDE,
the finale of Harlequin Desire's
DYNASTIES: THE LASSITERS *series.*
The terms of her father's will tore Angelica Lassiter
and her fiancé apart. But will their best friends'
wedding reunite them?

"**I** shudder to think how far you'd go to get what you wanted."

His expression tightened. "Yeah? Well, we both know how far you'll go, don't we?"

It was a cutting blow. When her father's will left control of Lassiter Media to Evan, it had resulted in an all-out battle between the two of them. Even now, when they both knew it had been a test of her loyalty, their spirits were battered and bruised, their relationship shattered beyond repair.

"I thought I was protecting my family," she defended.

At the time, she couldn't come up with any explanation except that her father had lost his mind, or that Evan had brazenly manipulated J.D. into leaving him control of Lassiter Media.

"You figured you were right and everyone else was wrong?" His steps toward her appeared automatic. "You slept in my arms, told me you loved me, and then accused me of defrauding you out of nearly a billion dollars."

All the pieces had added up in her mind, and they had been damning for Evan. "Seducing me would have been an essential part of your overall plan to steal Lassiter Media."

"Shows you how little you know about me."

"I guess it does."

Even though she was agreeing, the answer seemed to anger him.

"You *should* have known me. You should have trusted me. My nefarious plan was all inside your suspicious little head. I never made it, never mind executed it."

"I had no way of knowing that at the time."

"You could have trusted me. That's what wives do with their husbands."

"We never got married."

"Your decision, not mine."

They stared at each other for a long moment.

"What do you want me to do?" she finally asked, then quickly added, "About Kayla and Matt's wedding?"

"Don't worry. I know you'd never ask what I wanted you to do about us."

His words brought a pain to Angelica's stomach. He was up there on his pedestal of self-righteous anger, and she was down here…missing him.

Don't miss
REUNITED WITH THE LASSITER BRIDE
by Barbara Dunlop.

Available September 2014 wherever
Harlequin® Desire books and ebooks are sold.